A New Beginning in Coventry Beach

A New Beginning in Coventry Beach

Darlene Duncan

First Paperback Edition © 2022 Darlene Duncan
ISBN: 978-0-9723324-6-0

Published by Ocean Breeze Publishing

This novel and its characters are a product of the author's
imagination. Some locales may be factual but are used fictitiously.

To Charlotte, the love of my life,
my biggest fan and with whom
all things are possible.

CHAPTER 1

Standing on the shore watching the waves I closed my eyes and took a deep breath. The smell of coming rain mingled with the salty air. The distant thunder should have sent me running up the sandy path to the safety of the house, but it didn't. The wind picked up and my shirt billowed out in front of me. A bolt of lightning streaked across the sky and struck somewhere at sea.

Damn you, Rachel! Damn you for leaving me alone!

"Why?" I yelled at the ocean. Despite knowing that there would be no answer, I threw open my arms, tilted my head back and screamed out her name, "Raaaaachchchchelelelelel."

The tears streaming down my face were indistinguishable from the rain that was beginning to fall. This was the first time, since her death, that I had allowed myself to cry. Now as I had feared – I was unable to control the sobs that shook my body. Tears flowed freely. Breathing became difficult and I dropped to my knees, sat back on my heels, and again threw my arms wide, as I gasped out the words that I had intended to be a shout. "Here I am. Come and take me."

The lightning and thunder were the perfect visual and audio effects for the moment.

Exhausted, I slouched forward as huge raindrops came down like a sheet of water. Defeated and tired I got to my feet and turned from the ocean. Rivers of beach sand ran down my body as the rain continued to pour down on me.

Despite the rain, sand clung to my feet as I trudged up the narrow path to the house.

The house Rachel had always wanted.

I left the sliding glass door open, moved through the kitchen, turned on the Keurig, and headed upstairs for a hot shower.

Barefoot, dressed in light cotton lounge pants and a t-shirt, I put some honey in the bottom of a mug. While the hot water from the Keurig filled the cup, I swirled it around to quickly dissolve the honey. Once it was half-full, I dropped in a tea bag.

The storm had blown out to sea and night had moved in to replace it. Sitting on the screened in deck, I moved my chair from under the covered section, and looked up at the stars.

One of the great things about turtle season is the lack of ambient light at the beach. I leaned my head back and watched the twinkling night diamonds. With my hands wrapped around the tea mug, I took a long breath of the night air laced with sea salt and tea.

I set the mug on a small plastic table. Put my elbows on my knees and hung my head. The tears were starting again. They began to seep out the corners of my eyes. Roughly I wiped them away.

"Enough of this nonsense. She's been...gone for eighteen months. I can't spend the rest of my life crying over her. I..."

Meow.

"Huh?"

Meow.

I lifted my head and looked toward the sound.

Loud and demanding came another meow. The turtle nesting season approved floor lamp provided minimal illumination. I stood up and crossed the six feet to the screen door. Even though the small furry creature was right at the door, I could just barely make it out. Set in the face of a solid black cat were the most beautiful green eyes.

I opened the door and before I could reach down to pet the small cat, it was inside, and sitting in my chair. I smiled and with my hands on my hips looked at the little beast. "Well, why don't you just make yourself at home? As if you hadn't already."

I scooped up the small furball, and sat down, placing it in my lap. Sipping my tea, I petted the cat. "No collar. You look fairly well-fed and your fur is soft, and you're dry so you must have been inside when the storm blew through. You most likely belong to someone around here." I looked at the time. "I'm certainly not going around knocking on doors at this hour and I'm not turning you loose to roam the streets." The cat purred as it bathed itself in my lap. "Looks like we're having a slumber party."

After some searching, I found a square dish pan that I put some beach sand into, to use as a litter box. I set out a bowl with water as I told my guest, "Sorry, no cat food. Water will have to do until we find your people."

Having finished my nighttime ablutions, I came out of the bathroom to find my new feline friend was curled up on the pillow next to mine. A large smile covered my face. It was a facial expression that felt odd. It was my first real happy smile in an exceedingly long time.

I turned out the lights, opened the vertical blinds, and sank into the mattress. I placed a hand on the cat and fell asleep rubbing the top of its head.

CHAPTER 2

In the morning I visited some of the nearby houses asking about the cat. Several people said there was a stray that looked like the picture I had on my phone and a few of them even admitted to putting out food and water for it; however, no one claimed it as their own.

When I returned to the house, I found that my feline guest had come downstairs and was lounging in the recliner in the living room. At least I won't have to go upstairs to get him, I thought as I opened my laptop and began searching for a nearby vet clinic. Finding a place called The Cat House, I woke the cat.

As I scooped him up, I said, "I do hope you know how to behave in a car your majesty because I don't have a carrier on hand."

It was nice to have someone to talk to, even if it was just a cat.

I climbed into the SUV and after closing the driver's side door, I placed the cat on the front passenger seat, and waited. He sat and looked at me for a moment, blinked his mesmerizing green eyes a time or two, moved in a circle on the seat a few times, and laid down.

"So, you like riding shotgun, which means I'm not driving Miss Daisy, I'm driving… His Majesty King Tut." I pushed the remote for the garage door.

The cat turned his head and looked at me as if to say, "Are we going somewhere or are we just going to sit in the car?"

Although his coloring was solid black, his head had the triangular shape of a Siamese cat, reminding me of pictures I had seen of the ancient cats of Egypt.

"Yes, your majesty, we're going to the vet's office to have you scanned for a chip. I don't know what your name is, but I'm going to call you King Tut, Tut for short." I heard his purr increase in volume, as if he were giving approval to the name.

In the parking lot of The Cat House, I spoke to the cat, acting as if he understood what I said, "All right, Tut." He stretched himself and sat up, looking at me. "We're here now and I don't want any shenanigans out of you. I don't have any idea what other critters are inside. Regardless, you need to maintain your regal behavior."

The cat allowed himself to be picked up and carried inside the building. Once inside he began to wiggle a bit and I tried to contain him, but his lithe body and slick fur made him difficult to control. Before I knew it, he had climbed up on my shoulder and draped himself around my neck like a scarf. His front legs hanging down one side of my chest and his back legs down the other.

The young lady behind the counter watched the entire thing with virtually no reaction. She acted as if every cat that came through the door behaved in this way. "Good morning. Welcome to The Cat House. I'm Sheryl. How can I help you?"

"Hi, Sheryl." I stepped up to the high counter. "I need to have him" I pointed at the cat around my neck "scanned for a chip. He showed up at my place last night. I've checked with the neighbors and no one seems to know to whom he belongs."

The young lady studied the cat as if he looked familiar, after several moments she shrugged and with a smile said, "Sure thing." She pointed to her left where the countertop was waist high instead of chest high. "If you'll place him over here. I'll be able to do that for you."

5

I reached up, removed my feline scarf, and placed him on the counter. He sat down and glanced up at me with a look of tolerant disdain. I got the impression that he was humoring me. It was as if he were saying, "Poor silly human. Don't you know who I am?"

Sheryl held a device in her hand that looked like a large magnifying glass, except the circle that should have held the glass was empty. She ran the device over Tut's body and within a few seconds there was a beep, and Sheryl looked down at the number. She scratched the cat on top of his head and said, "See that wasn't so bad." He pushed her hand with his head.

Back at the high counter Sheryl entered the number from the scanner. Seconds later she said, "I thought you looked familiar, Sir Reginald."

I smiled, rubbed the cat's ears, and said, "I knew you were royalty, my friend." Looking up at the vet's assistant I continued, "If possible, I'd like to deliver him to his people."

"Let me just call the owners and make sure that's all right." She looked up the owner's record in her computer and with a slight frown said, "Well, Sir Reginald it looks like you're about a year overdue for your shots." She picked up the desk phone and punched in the numbers.

I could hear it ringing and then a voice came on saying the number had been disconnected. "Looks like we may have a hard time finding your people fella."

Sheryl was staring at her computer screen looking uncertain about what to do next, when I offered, "Tell you what, I'll leave my contact information with you and when you figure out how to get in touch with his people, you can give them my information."

This brought a smile to the young lady's face and she put a pad and pen on the counter. As I pushed the pad back to Sheryl I said, "I just moved in, so I have some shopping to do and since it looks like I'll have a feline house guest for at least a little while my first stop will be the pet store."

The young lady read my information and asked, "Are you trying to be funny?"

With a confused look on my face, I asked, "I don't understand. What's the problem?"

"The problem is that you wrote down the address for Sir Reginald's owner. If you knew where he lived all along, what was this all about?"

"Huh? I assure you I'm not..." I paused. "Is the owner's name Martha Wilcox?"

Sheryl opened her mouth, most likely to make a smart-ass reply. Something about my expression must have told her that that wasn't a really good idea. She closed her mouth, cleared her throat, and said, "Yes. How..."

I swallowed hard. "Martha Wilcox died almost two years ago. That's when I bought the house. I've been leasing it out but decided to spend the summer in it." I looked at the cat and said, "Sorry old man. Looks like your person is gone." Musing out loud to myself, "What have you been doing with yourself for the past two years?"

The cat pushed his head against my chest and then placed his front paws on my shoulders and head butted my chin. Placing my hands on his body under his front paws I picked him up and held him, so we were eye-to-eye. "You and me?" I paused. "Yeah, you and me."

When I left the vet's office Sir Reginald's name had officially been changed to King Tut, he was up to date on all his shots, and the microchip showed me as his new owner. Though both of us knew that I was more Staff than owner.

Before we returned home, we paid a visit to the local pet supply store, where I picked up all the necessities and a few extras to make my new companion's life easier.

Entering the beach house through the garage I put my purchases on the kitchen counter. Then I filled the food dish and the water fountain and placed them on the floor at the end of the counter.

Leaving Tut to eat in peace, I opened the sliding glass door and took a deep breath of the humid air, laced with salt, and seaweed. The breeze coming off the water was refreshing. There was no way it could be called cool, yet it wasn't like the hot winds that occasionally blew across the state from the west picking up heat as they moved across the land. I left the sliding glass door open enough that the cat could get out to join me when he finished eating.

It wasn't long before Tut jumped into my lap and began grooming himself.

I sighed and said, "Seems you and I have something in common. Your person died too." I took a deep breath and let it out slowly. "I hope you approve of your new name, your majesty. Not sure how you've been surviving on your own for almost two years. In any case, as long as I have a home so do you my feline friend." I put my hand under his chin and looked into Tut's green eyes, "Who knows maybe we'll keep this place. What do you think?"

Tut pushed on my hand with his head and meowed. I smiled. "Yes, I agree."

CHAPTER 3

For eighteen months after Rachel's death, I traveled the country. Never stayed in one place more than a few weeks. I needed to not be alone, but I wasn't interested in a long-term relationship. Not of the platonic or the romantic variety.

After days of being alone with only Tut for company I decided to seek out people. A little research on the internet led me to a gay bar in Central City, Greta's.

I paid the cover charge and stepped into the crowded club. The music was loud, and the dance floor was crowded. At first glance it was hard to tell who was dancing with who. Looking a little closer, I could see the men were dancing with men and the women were dancing with women and I knew I was in the right place.

Even if I didn't find any companionship here, at least I was around people. I needed that feeling of belonging.

At the bar I ordered a club soda with a twist of lime. I had no intention of drinking anything stronger. I handed the bartender a ten and walked away.

I took a sip of my drink and wandered to the game room in the back. It was a large building and the game room provided ample space for the two pool tables and the half-dozen video games on the end wall. Among the electronic games was a sit-down version of Ms. Pac-Man.

Rachel loved playing Ms. Pac-Man.

I pushed away the memories that threatened to overwhelm me. I watched a couple arguing at the pool table furthest from the games.

Standing against the wall between the two pool tables, I listened. It seemed that the blonde was accusing the brunette of cheating, and not at pool. The brunette didn't need to say a word - guilt was written all over her face.

The petite blonde slammed her pool cue into the wall rack and stalked out of the room, making a beeline for the bar. I followed her.

"Bourbon and make it a double."

Coming up behind her I signaled the bartender that I would pay for her drink and held up my glass. "And I'll have another."

I stepped up next to the young woman. "Hi, I'm Laurel. Is it always this crowded in here on a weeknight?"

Blondie accepted the drink from the bartender downed it and demanded another. She turned to me, looked me up and down, and smiled. "Sara." She scanned the room, her eyes stopped on the brunette she'd been chewing out. Then she looked at me. "Yes, it is rather crowded tonight. How about we go someplace less crowded?"

"Why not?" I placed my glass on the bar with a one-hundred-dollar bill.

As we stepped into the warm night air I asked, "Where would you like to go?"

Her response was to turn to me and pull my head down so our lips could meet. She delivered a passionate kiss. I could feel my body responding. My heart raced and my breathing became much more rapid. When we broke from the kiss she whispered, "Anywhere we can be alone."

The door to my room at the Super 8 was barely closed when Sara wrapped herself around me and gave me another passionate kiss.

I pulled her closer to me and let my hands roam her back, but before I could unhook her bra, she pulled away.

Chewing on her lower lip and breathing heavily she said, "I don't think I can do this."

Taking a deep breath and smiling I said, "No worries." Turning away from her I moved to the cooler of drinks I'd put in the room earlier. "Soda?"

"Look, I'm real sorry. I just..."

I opened a bottle of ginger ale and turned to face her. "You just wanted to make her feel as bad as she made you feel." She looked confused. I sat down in one of the two chairs in the room. "I overheard your conversation by the pool table."

"Oh."

Screwing the top back on the soda bottle I stood up. "How about if I drive you back to Greta's?"

Sara looked at me as if she were trying to figure something out. "What?"

"Why are you being so nice? I come on to you and then shut you down and you..." She threw her hands up and plopped down on the edge of the bed.

Laughing I said, "Everybody makes mistakes. How long have you two been together?"

"Going on two years." Sara was staring at the floor.

"Do you love her?"

She lifted her head and looked me in the eyes. "Yes."

"Then let me take you back to the club. Hopefully, she's still there."

"It's not that far. I can walk back."

"True, it's not far. It's also true that it's not exactly the best of neighborhoods. I drove you from there and I'll drive you back."

We put the cooler into the car and headed back to Greta's. I dropped Sara off at the front door and wished her, good luck. She thanked me and went inside.

CHAPTER 4

After the drama of my visit to Greta's, I was content with my peaceful life at the beach. Maybe I would go back there some day but for now life with Tut was perfect.

The days passed and I could feel a tension I hadn't realized was there, begin to leave my body.

I began thinking about the upgrades and minor remodeling that Rachel and I had discussed when we purchased the house. The first one that I took care of was upgrading the screening on the back deck.

The first night Tut and I tried to sit out and enjoy the evening, the no-seeums kept finding their way through the mesh of the screening. For that night, we moved to the second-floor balcony, where the breeze was strong enough to keep the tiny pests at bay.

The next day I called a screen company and had the screening replaced with a tighter weave screen. I left the second-floor balcony unscreened, the breeze at that height was usually strong enough to keep the bugs away, and I preferred the unobstructed view.

Ever since Tut came into my life I sleep much better, although this morning I woke a couple of hours before sunrise and decided to stay up for Mother Nature's morning show.

No two sunrises at the beach are the same. On mornings without any clouds, Sol lays a river of gold from the horizon to the sand. Those days with a few clouds can be much more colorful. The number of clouds and their composition change the way the white light of the sun is scattered, and create magnificent, although short-lived works of art.

Sitting in the chair next to me, Tut was grooming himself. I listened to the sound of the palm fronds and the rounded leathery leaves of the Sea Grapes as the ever-present sea breeze pushed the plants against each other adding to the soothing sounds of the waves rolling ashore. The only sound of civilization was the gurgling of the coffee pot coming from inside the house.

I took a deep breath of the sea air, looked at Tut, and smiled as I remembered how quickly he had become accustomed to the harness and leash. "I don't know why you came into my life, your majesty, but I'm certainly happy to have you."

Walks on the beach were much more entertaining with Tut along. He chased Sandcrabs, ignoring the waves that soaked him as he tried to dig up the crabs. I laughed, and told him, "Sorry to tell you old man, but they can dig up to four feet down. I don't think you're going to catch one."

The first time I found myself laughing at the cat's antics, the sound surprised me. Tears flowed from my eyes as I realized I hadn't laughed since Rachel's death. Ignoring the fact that Tut was soaking wet, I scooped him into my arms and holding him close to me said, "You sir, are a balm for my soul."

I quickly learned that every fisherman along the shore knew Tut and most of them had fed him during his days on the loose.

I glanced over at the feline who was performing his grooming ritual. It still amazed me that he had hung around the house of his previous owner, surviving as best he could and then attached himself to me when I moved in. "Your majesty, you are one unique cat."

Shortly after adopting Tut, I realized that perhaps Martha Wilcox's heirs wanted the cat. I contacted the real estate agent who had handled the sale of the house and explained the situation. When the agent got back to me and she assured me that Mrs. Wilcox's family had no interest in claiming the cat, I breathed a sigh of relief. I had already decided that if they wanted the cat, I would pay whatever price they wanted to let me keep him.

I stood up. The gurgling of the coffee maker had stopped. "I'll be right back, my furry friend."

He held his tail in a paw and looked from it to me as if to say, "Okay, don't be long." Then he returned to his ritual grooming.

I stepped inside and filled a thermos with the fresh brewed pot of French Vanilla coffee. What was left in the glass carafe went into my thermal mug. Loaded with the elixir of life I returned to the porch.

I set the thermos, thermal mug, and my 9mm Smith & Wesson on the small table next to my chair. Once I was comfortable, I patted my leg and Tut immediately moved onto my lap.

Absentmindedly rubbing the cats head, his purr meshed with the other sounds of nature. I drew a deep breath of the sea air and let it out slowly, as I reached for my coffee mug. Snap! Something or more likely someone had stepped on a twig or something similar.

Tut stopped purring and sat up. His attention was angled to the north. Without looking at the table I retargeted my reach so that my hand rested on the Smith & Wesson, instead of the coffee mug. Every few seconds Tut would flick his left ear.

Keeping my eyes focused on the darkness outside I asked, "Who's out there? Show yourself." The sound of me pulling the slide back on the 9mm Smith & Wesson was clearly audible on the still pre-dawn air.

A female voice called out, "Don't shoot. My name is Carly Reddington. My Aunt Martha owns this house." Silence and then, "Or at least I thought she did."

There were more noises of rustling among the foliage and a young woman stepped up to the screening, close enough to be seen in the faint light put out by the red-light bulb of the small lamp I kept on the deck.

"Are you alone?"

The young woman smiled. "Just me and my shadow."

I unlocked the door, stepped back, and said, "Come in." My visitor looked at the gun in my hand and hesitated.

It was my turn to smile. "You can come inside, or you can wait right there being eaten alive by the bugs while we wait for the police to arrive."

I knew that as long as she was moving the bugs weren't too bad but standing still the no-seeums would make her life miserable. The young woman slapped the back of her neck.

"Yes, I see what you mean about the bugs. Hmmm, eaten alive for sure or perhaps shot." She shrugged, opened the screen door, and stepped inside.

"What did you say your name was?"

There was the slightest hesitation before she answered, "Carly Reddington. And you are?"

"The woman with the gun. Tell me why you're lurking around in the bushes at this hour."

Before she could reply Tut pulled the woman's attention away from me as he wove his way between her legs and meowed. The young woman looked down. "Sir Reginald, is that you? My goodness, but you've grown. The last time I saw you, you were just a handful." She scooped up the cat, holding him close to her, she buried her face in his fur and inhaled deeply. "A handful of Pistachio nut, thieving, kitten."

Still holding the cat, she sat down in the chair next to mine, Tut's chair. Tut stayed on her lap as she petted him. "You know I grew

16

up around here. It's a small town and the cops don't take this long to respond to a call." She pulled her eyes up from the cat in her lap and looked at me. "So, my guess is that you haven't actually called them." She looked back down at the cat in her lap. Her voice barely audible she asked, "Where's Aunt Martha?"

I studied the young woman. Mid to late twenties. Sun kissed blonde hair, blue eyes. The blue of the Caribbean on a clear sunny day. The bright yellow of her blouse enhanced her eyes, and the sand-colored shorts contrasted with the copper of her tan legs. A small straight nose, high cheek bones, and a strong chin. The combination was stunning. I gave myself a mental slap to remind me that I knew nothing about this woman, other than her supposed relation to the now deceased Martha Wilcox.

I've often said that animals are a good judge of character and Tut does seem to like her and she did know his previous name.

Regardless, I wasn't inclined to answer her question. "You still haven't told me why you were lurking about in the bushes. Why would you feel the need to sneak up on a house owned by a relative?"

Rubbing Tut's ears and looking out at the white surf just barely visible in the gray of coming sunrise, she replied, "Aunt Martha's dead, isn't she?"

I sat down and looking at the young woman, said, "Yes. Close to two years now."

She met my gaze and stood up, placing the cat in the chair. "I'm sorry I intruded on your solitude." She started for the screen door.

My words stopped her. "You still haven't answered my question."

She paused at the door and turned around. "Honestly, I was afraid that she was...gone. Somehow, I couldn't bring myself to ring the doorbell and have someone tell me that..., as I stood on the doorstep." Her gaze swept through the house and a slight smile crossed her face. "I'm not surprised that Jason and Janet sold the house. They never cared for the beach."

For some reason I couldn't state, I wanted to know more. I wanted to keep this woman talking. Maybe it was simply the loneliness of having only the cat to talk to since my arrival at Coventry Beach. "Where've you been that you didn't hear about your Aunts death?"

"Out of the country, traveling. I'm a Freelance Journalist. You never have told me your name."

"Laurel Carpenito." I paused and in the ensuing silence Tut meowed, as if to say I needed to inform our guest of his name change. "And while you knew him as Sir Reginald, since I was adopted by him, I've changed his name to King Tut."

Carly smiled and looked at Tut. "Yes, I suppose you are more of a King than a Sir." She looked back to me with a quizzical expression. "When did you buy the house?"

"Rach...I purchased the house shortly after your aunt's death." I stood up and asked. "Would you like a cup of coffee? I've just brewed a fresh pot."

Carly hesitated for a few seconds before finally saying, "I should go. I need to check in with my friends and crash. It was a long plane ride."

I was surprised by the disappointment I felt and yet part of me was also relieved. "Of course. Stop by again. Tut obviously likes you."

I locked the screen door behind her and watched her walk down the narrow sand path to the beach. She was quickly swallowed by the scrub brush and palmettoes, before emerging on the beach.

Her parting words about needing to "check in with her friends" came back to me and I wondered what friends would be waiting for her on the dark, pre-dawn beach.

And if she just got off a plane where's her luggage? There's something not right about that girl's story.

"Relative of your former person or not, she's not telling the whole truth about why she's roaming about at this hour."

The sleek black feline was weaving between my legs, then stopped, looked up at me and meowed. I chuckled, scooped the cat up into my arms, and returned to my chair.

Sipping my coffee, while Tut purred in my lap I waited for the sunrise, while I mentally reviewed the meeting with Carly Reddington.

As expected, the clear sky allowed the sun to spread its golden hue across the water to the shore as it rose above the horizon. It was going to be a hot day.

As soon as the gold faded, I placed Tut in the chair next to mine and brought my laptop out. A quick internet search showed me images of the freelance journalist Carly Reddington. I sighed as I had to admit that the woman I'd met, looked like the images presented by Google.

Still there was something about that entire encounter that bothers me.

CHAPTER 5

Natalie strolled down the beach enjoying the sound of the surf gently rolling ashore. The pre-dawn gray of the sky promised a hot day without a cloud anywhere. Her thoughts were on her childhood friend Carly, wondering if she knew her Aunt Martha was dead.

Where is Carly and why in the world did, I tell that woman I was Carly? I could have told her I was looking for Carly but... Oh well, it is what it is, and I can't go back and change it now. I always thought Carly would buy her Aunt's house. Certainly, Jason and Janet would have worked with her on a payment plan. It's not like either of them needed the money from the sale of the house. Damn! Maybe Aunt Martha left Carly some money. Where the hell is she? I figured she'd have been here by now.

A flash of light a short distance ahead on the beach caught Natalie's attention. She stopped and waited to see if it would repeat.

There it was again. Closer to the dunes than to the shore. Since the sea oats that grew in there were protected and it was where some of the gulls built their nests, she knew no one should be up there.

The light flashed again, and Natalie could tell it wasn't actually coming from within the dunes. It was coming from the soft sand, just beyond the hardpack.

Natalie angled west as she moved south. Even in the dark the orange netting used to mark turtle nests was visible and when she had to go around a marked nest, she knew what was happening a short distance down the beach.

She stopped to get her bearings before continuing. The light flashed again. This time it was directly in front of her.

They're robbing a nest! Bastards! She quickly moved into the sand dunes. Using them as cover she scrambled to get into a position west of the sporadic light flashes.

I'll get a picture of these bastards. I suppose I should call 911 and get the cops down here. I can't call from this close; they'll hear me. Then she remembered that the county had recently upgraded to be able to receive 911 text messages.

She looked around trying to determine her exact location on the beach. Lost in thought she hadn't been paying particular attention to where she was. Her plan, such as it was, had been to meander down the shore until sunrise and then find a place for breakfast. Stumbling upon the nest robbers changed all that. Natalie needed to know where she was, so she could tell the cops.

She looked north and counted the looming shadows of the tall buildings. Aunt Martha's house was one of the last houses before the towering condos and hotels. If she was right the building directly behind her was the third of the mammoth concrete beasts.

Peering over the dunes she watched the two men digging and laughing, picturing in her mind past hatchings she had witnessed with the tiny sea turtles scampering into the ocean. Knowing that this nest would never hatch, her anger grew with each sound of mirth from the men plundering the nest.

She texted 911 her location with a brief explanation of what was going on. She was happy that this new service was available in the area. Using the sand hills to shield the light from her phone she set the camera for night vision and began recording. She pushed the sea oats aside for a better view.

Ping! Natalie's phone notified her of a text message.

Shit! I forgot to silence this damn thing. Maybe they didn't hear it.

"What the hell was that? Was that your phone?" The male voice was gruff and sounded harsh.

So much for that idea.

"No. Mine's set to vibrate. Maybe it was yours." While his companions voice was less harsh, it still lacked any warmth.

"I left mine on the boat." He paused. "There's somebody else out here."

Before Natalie could decide her next move, she heard a vehicle approaching.

Great! It must be the Turtle Patrol, they're the only ones who would be out here on an ATV. Now at least I won't be outnumbered. There will be two of us and two of them. I just hope they're not armed.

Natalie stood up and moved down to the destroyed nest. Standing across the hole from the two men, she spoke to the new arrival. "Great, it's you. These two bastards have dug up this nest. Radio for a patrol car."

The two men looked from her to the ATV driver and back. It only took Natalie a heartbeat to realize her mistake.

Shit! They're in it together.

She started to run back to the dunes, but the soft sand worked against her and the turtle traitor used the four-wheel drive quad to cut her off.

CHAPTER 6

After putting away the groceries, Tut and I headed for the beach. It was almost sunset, and the nearby condos cast long shadows on the sand. My house, the one to the north and the one south of my vacant lot, were the shortest buildings in the vicinity. There was a vacant lot on the other side of the southern house. Beyond that were multi-story hotels and condo buildings. I tried to ignore the long shadows these rectangular monstrosities cast but it was hard to do.

The sun was below the top floor of each concrete monolith and as I walked along in the surf watching Tut chase the Sandcrabs, it was like moving in and out of an eclipse. The building shadows were deep, and the sand covered by those shadows was already losing the warmth it had collected from the day's sunshine.

Ahead I saw a large lump on the sand.

No doubt debris the outgoing tide left behind. I sighed. Or some slob from one of the hotels or condos left his garbage for the next tide to take out.

Had this lump been in one of the sunlit areas, I would have seen it for what it was a lot sooner. However, in the shadow of the twelve-story condo building it was simply a big lump.

As I drew closer the form began to take shape. I swallowed hard and pulled out my phone.

"911, what is your emergency?"

I took a deep breath and said, "I think I've found a body washed up on the beach."

There was a brief pause, and the male voice asked, "What kind of body, ma'am? Is this a whale, a dolphin..."?

His condescending tone agitated me and in my most sarcastic tone I replied, "Sure I called 911 to report a dead fish on the beach. It's a person, you twerp."

He cleared his throat. "There's no need for name calling, ma'am. Are you sure this, person, is dead? Perhaps they're simply passed out or sleeping."

I had turned away from body and now I turned back to see Tut sitting on the hip of the corpse, staring down at the face. Without hesitating I raced over and snatched the errant feline off the body. "Tut, you bad boy. Get off of..." I gasped, "Oh my..." My chest constricted and it was hard to breathe. For a moment, I buried my face in the cat's soft black fur and inhaled the warm pleasant aroma of salty cat.

The dispatcher was still trying to get me to respond to him. I heard his voice, but it wasn't really a voice to me, simply a distant buzzing sound. Finally, I looked at the phone in my hand, trying to identify what it was and then lifted it to my face. "Just send a patrol car." I looked around me to find a geographic landmark. "We're in front of the third twelve story condo building south of 12308 Atlantic Avenue."

I disconnected the call and stood staring at the face of Carly Reddington while I waited for the police to arrive.

CHAPTER 7

The red and blue lights of the patrol cars were visible for quite a distance. It looked like they were at the same location as the robbed nest.

Why they would be back tonight? Damn it! All those lights will be keeping any turtles from coming ashore tonight. They were here for a couple of hours this morning I can't imagine why they're back tonight. Of course, there is at least one other nest in that same area. Maybe something has happened to the other nest. Damn turtle egg thieves have been busy this season.

As Terri approached the crime scene tape, she turned off her vehicle and dismounted. At first, she thought it was odd that there weren't a bunch of looky-loos standing around, then she remembered.

The snowbirds have gone home, and though I think someone has rented the old Wilcox house, I haven't met them yet.

Terri glanced back toward the Wilcox house. She thought she had seen someone out on the deck around sunrise yesterday. I need to stop by and introduce myself to the new renters.

A deputy approached the tape. "Ma'am, may I ask what you're doing on the beach at this hour?"

Terri saw Detective Angela Murdoch approaching behind the young man. Before she could 'educate' Deputy Miller, Angela said, "It's all right Miller. I'll take care of this troublemaker."

Deputy Miller touched his finger to his forehead in salute. "Yes ma'am." He turned and walked away.

"Troublemaker, huh?"

Angela smiled. "Yeah, I have to take my fun where I can find it." She glanced back over her shoulder. "Nothing fun about this case."

"I take it Miller is a new guy?"

"Yeah." Angela sighed. "You would think part of their training would be about the Turtle Patrol."

"Where's this one from?"

Angela shrugged. "Somewhere in the Midwest, I think." She stared after him for a moment.

"You need to keep an eye on that one. He doesn't like you. You didn't see the look on his face when you spoke to him, but I did."

Murdoch harrumphed and almost smiled, as she replied, "Yeah, I'm afraid he'll have to get in line. Ninety percent of the department doesn't like me. The men because I'm female and the few women on the force" she shrugged "I don't know maybe they're afraid I'll make a pass at them."

It was Terri's turn to have a little fun. "Or maybe they're afraid you won't." Before Murdoch could respond Terri changed the subject. "What's going on here?" She pointed toward the dunes directly in line with the crime scene. "The nest up there was robbed last night. Your guys were here half the morning." Terri smiled. "Personally, I think they just wanted to hang out at the beach. There certainly wasn't any evidence to collect this morning I can't imagine you're going to find anything in the dark."

Det. Murdoch looked from Terri, to where she was pointing, to the location of the body, and back to Terri before replying, "No, I didn't know." She lifted the crime scene tape and ducked under it. "Let's go take a look."

The two women walked from the hardpack to the softer sand near the base of the dunes. Angela turned on her flashlight as they moved away from the lights of the crime scene. "Since you have a better idea of exactly where the nest is, or rather was, than I do, I want you to guide me. I'd like to approach it from the side."

Terri looked at Murdoch questioningly. Murdoch shrugged. "If there's any evidence to be preserved, it will most likely be in front of the nest."

"Got it." Terri glanced up at the condo and moved more to Murdoch's right as they continued toward the dunes. "I doubt you'll find anything other than the destroyed nest. I told you, your guys were out here this morning."

"Yes, but they were looking at the scene as a nest robbing. I'll be looking at it in relation to murder."

"Murder!" Terri stopped in her tracks and turned to face Murdoch.

"Yeah." Murdoch sighed. "I don't suppose telling you will do any harm to the investigation. I'm sure by now it's on the internet. A young woman's body was found on the beach at sunset."

Terri resumed pushing through the soft white sand toward the destroyed nest. "Who is it?"

"No idea, at this point."

Pointing at a hole in the sand Terri said, "That used to be a turtle nest."

Murdoch scanned the nearby dunes with her flashlight. She ran the light over the sea oats and spotted the orange plastic mesh that had been used to mark the now destroyed nest.

Terri saw it too. "The deputies from this morning left it there saying they'd never get any prints off it."

Murdoch moved her light back to the nest, which was now a gaping hole in the sand. The metal grate designed to keep racoons and such from getting to the eggs was missing. It was obvious that whoever had dug up the eggs was in a hurry. Several of the fragile

27

specimens were smashed in the sand, as if they had been stepped on.

"Why were deputies out here for this? This is the Florida Fish and Wildlife Agent's territory."

Terri shrugged. "I don't know, maybe Fish and Wildlife is short handed."

"Probably. What happened to the metal grate?"

Terri shrugged again. "I don't know we didn't find it."

Murdoch moved toward the orange mesh and heard something crunch under her foot. She lifted her foot and aimed the flashlight at the sand where she'd heard the sound. Brushing the sand off the item she said, "I'd say someone lost a phone out here." She pulled a pair of nitrile gloves and an evidence bag from a pocket. "We'll see if the lab can get anything from it."

Angela cupped her hands and called. "Miller." The young man turned toward her. "Expand that crime scene tape all the way to the building."

As the two women walked back toward Terri's ATV, Murdoch cautioned her, "I'd appreciate it if you would let the rest of your volunteers know about this." She gestured at the crime scene. "A woman was killed here, we don't know who she is, why she was here, or why she was killed." She paused. "Who reported the nest robbing?"

"I don't know you'd have to ask the deputies that were here this morning. I just assumed it was someone walking on the beach." Terri started to climb onto her ATV but stopped. "You say you don't know who this woman is."

"That's right. No ID on her and none of the guys here recognized her. Of course, none of them grew up around here." Murdoch held Terri's gaze for a moment before asking, "Would you be willing to see if you recognize her? I know you've been here a long time."

28

Terri's eyes moved from Murdoch to the shrouded body and then back to Murdoch. "Sure." She gulped in sea air. "If it will help you catch a killer, I'm willing to give it a shot."

Murdoch lifted the crime scene tape again and as they walked to where the body lay on the wet hardpack, she asked, "Have you ever seen a dead body before?"

"No."

Murdoch squatted down next to the covered corpse and glanced up at Terri, as if to ask if she was ready. Terri nodded and Murdoch lifted the damp sheet to reveal the young woman's face.

Terri was surprised that she wasn't more repulsed by the sight. "I didn't know what I had expected but it wasn't for the face to look so natural, as if she's simply resting." Terri bent over some and tilted her head to get a better perspective on the woman's face.

When she straightened up Murdoch covered the woman's face and stood up. "Do you know who she is?"

"I can't be certain but if I had to guess, I'd say, it's either Carly Reddington or Natalie Kramer." Terri gave a small nervous laugh. "Those two girls look enough alike to be sisters."

Terri turned and looked up the beach, then brought her eyes back to Murdoch. "You know Carly Reddington's aunt was Martha Wilcox." She paused. "Have you met the new renters?"

Murdoch moved her gaze from Terri to the house up the beach. "She's the one who found the body."

"Not good for the tourist trade, that's for sure."

Murdoch walked her friend back to her vehicle. "Thanks for being willing to help, Terri."

"Whatever I can do, Angela. Do you think it's connected to the nest robbery?"

"I don't know but until we catch whoever did this, I think it's a good idea if your patrols work in pairs, especially at night."

"Yeah. Sounds like a good idea. I'll spread the word."

Murdoch started back toward her crime scene. Terri called to her. "If you want to know who the deputies were, stop by the station and I'll give you a copy of the report."

Murdoch gave her a thumbs up and continued on her way.

CHAPTER 8

I sat on the screened porch waiting for the police to arrive to question me about the body on the beach. I was still debating with myself about whether to tell them that I knew, well I really didn't know the person, but I did know her name...Carly Reddington.

Had it only been the wee hours of this morning that the young woman had walked down the very path I was now staring at?

How far did she get before...before what? I have no idea how she died. Maybe it was an accident. Maybe she decided to go for a swim and got caught in a rip current. But she said she grew up around here, surely growing up around the beach she would have known how to escape a rip current. Too many maybes.

The front doorbell rang, and I moved an annoyed Tut from my lap to his own chair. At the front door I looked through the peephole and asked, "Who is it?"

A woman's husky voice answered, "Sheriff's Department, ma'am. Detective Murdoch." A gold badge filled the peephole, then was removed to show the woman at the door.

I opened the door and for a moment studied Det. Murdoch. She stood close to six feet tall, her short spiky hair looking as if she had just gotten out of bed, thick eyebrows over beautiful slate grey eyes. The dark circles under those eyes gave evidence of not enough sleep. The wide mouth with full lips looked inviting and I stifled a sudden desire to kiss them.

Hoping that the idea of kissing the sheriff's detective hadn't shown on my face, I said, "Please, come in detective. Can I get you a cup of coffee? There's always a fresh pot brewing." I headed to the kitchen leaving her to close the door and follow me.

"Yes, thank you. I take it black."

"Good thing, because I don't have anything to put in it." I tried my best to keep my voice friendly. "Unless you'd like a shot of Irish Whiskey in it."

"No thanks. I'm on duty."

I could feel her eyes following me. Something told me that I was once again a murder suspect. Unlike when Rachel's family accused me of murdering her, this time the woman in question may have actually been murdered. As I rounded the corner into the kitchen, I took a deep breath to calm myself. I schooled my expression to give away nothing of what I was feeling.

As I poured the coffee, I watched Det. Murdoch. She stood in the living room slowly examining everything before she casually walked to the breakfast bar and accepted the coffee cup.

"Thanks." Holding my gaze, she asked, "Is the artwork original?"

"Yes. They're all by a local artist. She uses reclaimed wood, mostly from fences destroyed by hurricanes."

I decided that Det. Murdoch had a good poker face.

"My favorite is Coventry Sunrise. Which one do you like the best?"

The detective turned back to the living room, scanning the art on the walls. She brought her gaze back to me and without answering my question, took a notebook from her pocket and asked, "Did you know the victim?"

It was my turn to not answer a question, as I still hadn't decided how I was going to answer that question. "Please, have a seat at the table. It will be much more comfortable." I pointed to the small round table in the breakfast nook. Without waiting for an answer, I walked out of the kitchen and sat at the table, with my back to the wall.

Once we were seated, Tut strolled in and jumped into my lap. He placed his two front paws on the round table and stared at Detective Murdoch.

With that expressionless poker face the detective repeated her question. "Did you know the victim?"

Rubbing the cat's head and ears, I held the detective's gaze. "Not really."

One of Det. Murdoch's eyebrows rose. It was easy to see she wasn't happy with the answer. I suppose she thought I wasn't taking the investigation seriously.

"You do understand that this is a murder investigation." She looked back and forth between the cat and me a few times.

"Yes, detective. I'm well aware of what this is about." I drew in a shaky breath. Then noticing the detective's attention to Tut, I said, "Yes, the short black hairs you found on the, body, most likely belong to Tut here." I hurried on. "While I was on the phone with your dispatcher, I turned my back on…, and when I turned around Tut was sitting on the body. I scooped him up and that's when I saw her face." I sipped my coffee. "It was Carly Reddington."

I told the detective about my encounter with Carly Reddington.

When I finished my story, Murdoch held my gaze for several seconds without speaking, then, "Why do I get the feeling you're not telling me everything?"

It occurred to me that perhaps I should tell the detective my real name. As quickly as the idea presented itself, I dismissed it.

I don't know her well enough to trust her. Just because she's a cop doesn't mean she's trustworthy.

"I've told you everything there is to tell." I took a sip of coffee. It was starting to get cold. "Would you like a warmup on your coffee, detective?"

There was the slightest hesitation before Det. Murdoch replied, "Yes, thank you. It's very good."

While I brought the thermos to the table and poured, Det. Murdoch again examined the room. "I'm curious. What does it cost to lease a place like this?"

As I screwed the top into the thermos, I smiled. "I wouldn't know. A friend of mine owns this place and she's letting me stay here for the summer."

"That's some friend. I know what these properties sell for. Can't be cheap to rent." She scribbled something in her notebook and then laid the pad on the table with the pen inside it, marking the page she was on.

Det. Murdoch sipped her coffee as she watched me sit back down. Seconds later Tut was again in my lap, paws on the table watching Det. Murdoch watch me. "Do you often take your cat for walks on the beach?" There was a slight lilt, almost a hint of laughter to that husky voice, as if she were amused by the idea of a cat being taken for a walk.

I scratched the top of Tut's head between his ears. "Yes, he and I spend a great deal of time on the beach. Usually, early morning and at sunset." I paused. "Though the sunset walks may stop, at least for a bit."

The detective's facial expression was deadpan as she said, "Are you aware that animals aren't allowed on the beach?"

Tut chose that moment to jump down and have a snack.

I fought to maintain my bland expression and said, "The signs say, "no dogs". I didn't see any mention of cats."

Neither of us spoke for a few heartbeats. The detective took another sip of her coffee.

"What time was this encounter with Carly Reddington?"

"Just before 4:00 a.m." I paused. "I woke early and decided to just stay up and watch the sunrise. We sit out there" I indicated the back deck "and listen to the surf. It's very relaxing."

"We? Oh, you mean the cat."

I bristled. "Yes, I mean the cat. Tut is a wonderful companion. Quiet, self-sufficient, he doesn't ask questions and he doesn't steal the covers at night." I stared at the woman before me as if challenging her to say something about my attachment to the cat and wondering why I told her the cat sleeps with me.

The detective held my gaze. "Why didn't you tell us earlier that you knew the victim?"

I didn't like the challenging tone in her voice. Honestly, I didn't like anything about her attitude. Being treated as a murder suspect wasn't my idea of fun.

Tut jumped back onto my lap and pushed on a hand. I dropped my gaze to the cat, began rubbing his ears as he lay down. He always seems to know when I need him. I smiled and looked back up at the detective and with a shrug said, "I wasn't sure I wanted to get any more involved in this than I already was. It's not every day that I find a dead person on the beach." I paused and then very quietly said, "I've had more than enough of death."

"Care to explain that last statement?"

The detective's question made me realize I must have made the last statement aloud. Crap! If I tell her about Rachel's death, then it won't take her long to figure out my real name and I'd just as soon she didn't. Though if she's any good at her job it won't take her long to figure out my real name anyway.

35

"No, I don't." I pulled Tut into my arms and stood. "As a matter of fact, if you have any further questions you can contact my lawyer." While I spoke, I draped the cat around my neck, grabbed the detective's coffee cup, removed a thermal travel mug from the cabinet under the breakfast bar, and poured Det. Murdoch's coffee into the travel cup. Handing it to her, I said, "Goodnight, detective."

She took her time tucking her notebook into a pocket, rose, and accepted the proffered cup. "As you wish." She handed me a business card. "In case you think of anything you want" she emphasized the last word "to tell us, here's my contact information." At the front door she turned and asked, "Who's your lawyer?"

I sighed. "Well, I suppose I'll have to get one. As soon as I do" I waved the detective's business card "I'll be certain to have them contact you. Good night, detective." I closed the door in her face, just as she lifted the coffee cup in a salute. Through the closed door I heard a muffled, "Thanks for the coffee."

CHAPTER 9

Sitting at her desk Detective Angela Murdoch began searching the internet for anything she could find on Laurel Carpenito. She started her search with the county property appraisers' site to learn who owned the house Laurel Carpenito was calling home. The records showed that Larissa Carpenter and Rachel Simmons were the owners and they paid cash. Remembering the connection Terri Snokes had mentioned between the victim and the previous owner of the house, Murdoch opened another search window. She found that Martha Wilcox had died of natural causes a few weeks before the two women bought the place.

A quick search on Larissa Carpenter and Rachel Simmons took her to several news articles about the couple winning the biggest lottery jackpot in the state's history. Shortly after that win Rachel Simmons died.

At first, she found it interesting that Larissa Carpenter had been a suspect in Rachel Simmons' death. Further reading showed that those pushing that theory were basically family members of the deceased. Several articles were about how the family felt that Larissa Carpenter had tricked Rachel into marrying her and now she was not only listed as sole beneficiary on the life insurance policy, but she also inherited Rachel's share of the lottery jackpot. An autopsy determined that Rachel Simmons had died of natural causes, a brain aneurysm.

Before Murdoch could start a search for images of Laurel Carpenito, Larissa Carpenter, and Rachel Simmons, her desk phone rang. The light indicated it was an interdepartmental call. Having requested confirmation of the deceased's identity through fingerprints, she hoped this was her answer.

She picked up the receiver. "Murdoch."

"Yeah, I don't know who told you that your beach body was Carly Reddington, but they lied."

"All right we know who she isn't. Do we know who she is?"

"We got a hit on a Natalie Kramer. She's a local kid."

"Great. What about the phone I gave you?"

"We're working on it. Fortunately, I don't think it was out there very long. Of course, it would be easier if you hadn't stepped on it."

"Yeah, but if I hadn't stepped on it. It would still be out there under the sand. By the way, why did we have Natalie Kramer's prints on file?"

"What? You want me to do all the work?" She could hear the smile in Paul's voice and then the call ended.

A quick records search showed that Natalie Kramer had been arrested for protesting without a permit when she was nineteen. Murdoch pulled up the case file.

Natalie Kramer wasn't the only one arrested that day. Carly Reddington had been charged with the same thing.

Reading through the list of names charged that day she smiled, as she came across several local resident's names, including Terri Snokes from the Turtle Patrol.

Sitting at her desk doodling and thinking, she tried to fit the pieces of the puzzle together. After a few moments she dropped the pen and picked up the Rubik's Cube. Staring across the room with unseeing eyes she began to go through all the facts, possible lies, and conjecture of the case, while randomly turning the pieces of the cube.

There's no obvious reason for Carpenito to lie about her meeting with Natalie Kramer, so why would Natalie Kramer say her name was Carly Reddington? Though I suppose if she had been caught poking around in the wee hours it made more sense if she were the former owner's niece. Still, none of that makes any sense at all. Somehow, some way, the turtle nest, Natalie Kramer, and Carly Reddington are all tied together. I just have to figure out the common thread and where Laurel Carpenito fits into the picture.

CHAPTER 10

After the detective left, I debated with myself about actually getting an attorney. After debating the pros and cons, the simple fact that I told the detective I would be getting an attorney convinced me I needed to get one.

I haven't done anything illegal. Yeah, like that'll make a difference.

Eventually, I texted the lawyer Rachel and I had used to help us deal with our lottery winnings. I didn't expect an immediate response as it was almost midnight. However, shortly after I sent my text, my phone rang. It was our attorney, Jacob Smythers. I gave him a rundown on the situation and asked him for a referral to a criminal defense attorney.

First thing in the morning, I called to make an appointment with the lawyer Mr. Smythers had recommended. Luck was with me and Earl James Davis had an unexpected opening that same morning.

I double checked that all the doors and windows were locked before leaving for my appointment. Tut was napping in the large recliner we often shared. At the door leading to the garage, I looked back to make certain the house was secured.

*　　*　　*　　*

The lawyer's office was upstairs in an older part of downtown. The building was many decades old and reminded me of the kind of building where private detectives, in old black and white movies, had their offices.

I was fifteen minutes early for my appointment and the receptionist asked me if I wanted something to drink. I declined. The young lady then suggested I have a seat that Mr. Davis would be with me shortly.

Despite her apparent youth the young lady, exhibited the efficiency and professionalism of a much older woman. Watching her, I was reminded of scenes from an old television series, Perry Mason. As I watched the young woman go about her duties, I mused to myself that she was a modern version of Perry Mason's efficient Secretary, Della Street.

At the exact moment of my appointment Mr. Davis stepped out of his office and greeted me.

"Good morning, Ms. Carpenito. Please, step into my office." The soft drawl of his words marked him as southern, rather than a transplant.

The reception area where I had waited was sparsely, yet comfortably furnished. When I stepped into Mr. Davis' private office the first thing I noticed, was the warmth. It wasn't the cold modern look of glass and steel I expected after experiencing his reception area. The L-shaped desk looked as if it were made of mahogany or some other dark wood. The well-worn, high-backed chair behind it looked like it would need replacing soon. The bookshelves on the wall behind the desk were full of law books, new and old, as well as a variety of books on topics related to living near the ocean. Turtles, ecology, marine life, and preservation of the dunes were a few of the topics I noticed. On the dark brown cork that covered the walls were colorful paintings of beach scenes and sea life.

I took a seat in one of the bucket chairs rather than on the sofa. Unlike some other chairs of its type this one wasn't so large that it

41

was uncomfortable. It was roomy without swallowing me, allowing me to sit up straight and keep my feet on the floor. I rested my arms on the sloped curve from the back that created the chair arms.

Before taking a seat, Mr. Davis said, "Would you like a drink? A bottle of water? Tea? Coffee?"

I started to decline the offer and then changed my mind. My throat was suddenly quite dry. "Yes, a bottle of water would be nice. Thank you."

I watched as he moved to the small refrigerator on the far side of the room. It was obvious he had once been very athletic and while I noticed he was starting to get a bit thick around the middle he still had a tight butt.

In short order, all the amenities were taken care of and Mr. Davis was sitting across from me with his own bottle of water.

"Where should I begin?"

"The beginning is usually the best place to start." My first instinct was to call him a smart-ass.

His boyish smile caused me to pause and he said, "After you set up your appointment, I contacted the referring lawyer. Jacob Smythers is an old friend from law school. He gave me a brief run down on the situation, but I need to hear it from you." He leaned toward the table that was between us and pushed a button on a digital recorder. "Unless you object, I'd like to record our conversation. It helps me when I need to refresh my memory about the facts of a case."

I shrugged. "Sure."

He said the date and time and then, "Initial meeting with Laurel Carpenito, referred to me by Jacob Smythers." His finger brushed a dial on the front of the device as he sat back in his chair. "Ms. Carpenito, please tell me what has brought you to me. Why do you think you need a criminal defense attorney?"

I took a swig of water and placed the bottle on the table in front of me. I took a long, slow breath of the cool recycled air. "First of all, my real name is Larissa Carpenter. I use the alias of Laurel Carpenito because everybody and his cousin knows that Larissa Carpenter is richer than Croesus."

The only reaction from Mr. Davis was a slight smile.

Odds are Mr. Smythers already told him my real name and he's pleased to see I trust him enough to tell him the truth.

His warm brown eyes and attentive expression made him easy to talk to and in no time at all I had told him everything, including my less than stellar opinion of local law enforcement.

Mr. Davis' expression never changed throughout my recitation, and he didn't interrupt me. As soon as I finished, he asked, "Do you know that the sheriff's department has identified the body on the beach as Natalie Kramer?"

At first, I was confused, then suspicious. "How do you know that?"

He smiled but didn't answer my question. "Do you know anyone named Natalie Kramer?"

I thought for a moment. "No, the name doesn't ring any bells for me. Why would this Natalie Kramer claim to be Carly Reddington?"

Mr. Davis took a sip from his water bottle. "Natalie Kramer and Carly Reddington grew up together. They were best friends." He smiled. "And they looked enough alike to pass for twins."

Throughout the meeting I had been studying Mr. Davis. His face looked quite familiar. "Did you go to school with Rachel Simmons?" I leaned forward a bit, with my elbows resting on my knees. "Your face looks familiar to me." I tilted my head one way and then the other.

"Rachel Simmons." He said the name out loud and made a face as if dredging up an old memory.

I smiled. "Even if you didn't go to school with her. You already know her name from your research on me, don't you?"

"You're good." He returned my smile. "Yes, to both of your questions. I did go to school with Rachel and yes, her name came up when my assistant researched you." He paused. "How did you know that I went to school with her?"

"Rachel liked to flip through her senior yearbook every now and then. She always wanted to move back here, and she wondered if any of her old classmates would still be here." I paused and studied Mr. Davis for a moment. "If memory serves me, you were on the debate team with her.

He nodded his confirmation of my statement. "Rachel was quite popular with pretty much everyone in our class. I was sorry to hear of her passing." He glanced over my shoulder at the clock I knew was on the wall behind me and stood up. "From what you've told me you don't have anything to worry about. I'm sure Detective Murdoch will be back in touch with you. In the meantime, I'll let the detective know that you've retained me to represent you. If you feel uncomfortable or you just don't want to answer her questions, just tell her to call me."

CHAPTER 11

When I entered the house, everything looked the same, but something was off. It just didn't feel right. Standing in the doorway from the garage, I reached behind me and pulled the 9mm Smith & Wesson from its holster. Gun in hand I stepped into the house.

The sliding glass door to the screened in porch was open. I knew it was closed and locked before I left. The blinds were positioned so that I was unable to see if there was anyone on the deck.

Though I had never been a scout, I always believed in being prepared. I had entered Det. Murdoch's contact information into my phone in case I lost the card the detective had given me. I called the number and placed the phone on the dishtowel that was on the breakfast nook's table.

I left the door to the garage open. An open door would make a fast exit easier. "Whoever is out there, show yourself." I waited but the only response I got was Tut. He came wandering in through the open sliding glass doors and headed straight for the garage. I used my foot and closed the door before he could slip out. "Think you're quite the little escape artist, don't you?" I quietly said to the cat but never took my eyes off the open doorway to the porch. "I've already called the police – Carly."

With her hands in the air a young woman stepped into view. "How did you know it was me?"

It was like seeing a ghost. My god, she looks just like… Why in the world… I know the attorney said they looked alike but…I'll have to process all of this later.

I lowered my gun but kept it in my hand. "I didn't know. It was an educated guess."

"Educated guess? You'll have to explain that to me some day." Carly turned as if to leave via the screen door. "But right now, I don't have time..."

I leveled the gun at her again. "You're not going anywhere. I don't know what kind of game you're playing or why Natalie Kramer was here pretending to be you but I'm sure Detective Murdoch will have some questions for you."

"Detective Murdoch?" Carly turned back to face me. Her eyes moved nervously between my face and the gun I was pointing at her. "Why would the police want to talk to me?"

"Maybe you can tell them why Natalie Kramer was impersonating you?"

Carly raised an eyebrow. "Natalie? I didn't even know she was in town. I just got back myself." She paused. "How do you know she was impersonating me?"

I hesitated. "I caught her lurking around out back here, yesterday in the wee hours. She told me her name was Carly Reddington, the niece of the previous homeowner. Anyway, just before sunset yesterday, I nearly tripped over her body on the beach."

"What!?!" Carly's calm collected demeanor changed drastically. She reached out and grabbed the edge of the sliding glass door for support.

The door behind me, that I hadn't heard open, closed and a voice said, "You can lower the gun Ms. Carpenito. I don't think your intruder is going to run off." Det. Murdoch deposited Tut in my arms. "Your cat on the other hand tried to escape as I came in."

She walked past me and helped Carly to a chair in the breakfast nook.

I set Tut on the table, holstered my gun, and picked up my cell phone. Then I went to the kitchen and returned with a glass of water for Carly and a cup of black coffee for the detective.

Carly thanked me for the water and Detective Murdoch said, "I do hope you have a license for that gun."

My only response was to say, "I'll be on the deck if you need me for anything." At the sliding glass door, I paused, turned to look at Carly, and said, "I'm sorry for the loss of your friend."

The sounds of the surf, the breeze, and the gulls made it impossible to hear the brief conversation between the two women in the house.

Not that I want to know what they're saying anyway.

I sighed and rubbed Tut's ears. I closed my eyes and immersed my senses in the smells and sounds of the shore, the salty air, the rustling of the palmettos, the fussing of the sea gulls, and the humid heat of Florida in early summer.

My reverie was interrupted when Det. Murdoch stepped out to let me know that she and Carly were leaving.

"Are you going to press charges for breaking and entering?"

I took a deep breath of the sea air. "No, but you can tell her to get rid of her keys. The locks will be changed before sundown."

From behind Murdoch, Carly said, "I don't have a key; however, the garage door code hasn't been changed since I was a teenager."

CHAPTER 12

That night, like so many of the nights following Rachel's death, I was unable to sleep. Tossing and turning I tried to find that perfect position that would allow me to get to sleep. Surrendering to the insomnia I started to head downstairs for the screened in porch. A tightness in my chest grew with each step and part way down the stairs, I stopped. Looking down at Tut, who was standing on the step next to my feet, I said, "How about we opt for the balcony tonight?"

Tut looked at me on the dimly lit staircase as if to say, "Wherever you want to go, Mom. I'm with you."

The tightness in my chest eased with each step back to the second floor. As I opened the slider to the balcony the ocean breeze brought with it the salty aroma of the Atlantic Ocean. While it wasn't as cool as the air-conditioning of the house it was much more enticing. The outside air had substance and flavor to it as it carried the smells of nature to my nose.

The soft aroma of the Sweet Almond mixed with the fruitiness of the Rangoon Creeper combined with the salty sea air made me smile. The steady breeze kept the no-see-ums and the mosquitoes away and I settled into the lounge chair. I covered my bare legs with a lightweight blanket, which Tut quickly plopped himself on and began licking a paw and then wiped his face with that paw, in preparation for sleep.

It was still dark when I woke again. Wide awake, I listened, wondering if the sound that woke me was part of a dream or not.

Now in addition to the smells of nature, the ocean breeze carried angry voices. I reached for the binoculars I kept on the table next to the lounge chair. I moved a lever and the device converted to night vision. The scene on the beach was like a well-lit black and white movie.

Three people. Two women and a man. One of the women was leaning in toward the man and wagging a finger at him. Either the man was exceedingly short, or this woman was taller than average. She seemed to tower over him and everything about her body language screamed anger.

The other woman was standing to the side, watching. She was just a little bit of a thing, especially compared to the other woman. Her body language spoke of timidity and submission.

The man's posture told me he was used to be chastised and yelled at. There was no effort on his part to speak or defend himself in any way.

I felt like this might be a lover's spat and thought I shouldn't be spying on this couple, though I was a bit confused about why the third party was there. Perhaps, she was the third leg of the triangle. Still, it just doesn't seem right. Who would…?

Just as I was about of lower the binoculars, the angry woman's posture changed, and I hesitated.

What's she going to do now? This is like watching a train wreck.

The angry woman's left hand reached out and rested on the man's shoulder as her right arm came forward with such speed that I didn't realize what was about to happen until it had already happened.

She stabbed him! What the hell?

Unable to look away, I watched the man sink to the sand as the woman extracted the knife. Knife in hand she leaned over the body, curled in a fetal position, and wiped the blade on the man's shirt sleeve. Then she straightened up and walked away. The timid woman glanced down at the man's body as she walked past him to follow his killer. Neither of the women looked back.

My throat was so tight breathing was difficult and talking was impossible.

I don't know how long I remained frozen, looking at the heap on the sand before I grabbed my cell phone.

When Det. Murdoch answered the phone, I launched into what I had just seen, with no preamble of any kind. "I've just witnessed a murder on the beach in front of my house. They were standing there arguing and then she just stabbed him."

"Huh? Who?" There was a brief pause.

From the sound of her voice, it was obvious that the detective had been sound asleep.

"Ms. Carpenito? Slow down and repeat what you just said."

Murdoch's commanding tone helped me gain control, I took a deep breath, and repeated myself.

Murdoch ordered me to stay where I was and disconnected the call. Though I've never been good about taking orders, this time I had no desire to move from where I was.

CHAPTER 13

While she dressed, Murdoch called dispatch and had them send a patrol car and an ambulance to the beach in front of Laurel Carpenito's house.

As Laurel opened the door to Det. Murdoch, Murdoch's phone rang. In the distance, was the sound of an ambulance siren. Closing the door made the siren seem further away, but they both knew it was getting closer.

The detective looked at her cell phone. "Excuse me", she said to Laurel as she answered the phone. "What have you got Brighton?"

Murdoch heard the young deputy swallow hard. "A dead man." He paused. "He's in the fetal position, so I can't see any obvious wounds, but there's blood soaking into the sand. Looks like it came from his mid-section."

She moved through the house to the sliding glass doors that led to the deck. Standing on the deck she could tell by Brighton's stance that he was uncomfortable. A small smile of remembrance flashed across her lips as she remembered her first dead body.

"Is the tide coming or going?"

Murdoch knew Deputy Brighton was a surfer and would probably know the tide schedule and it would give him something to think about besides the corpse he was standing next to.

"It's coming in."

She swore under her breath. "Then we don't have much time. Use your phone to get as much of the crime scene photographed as possible. I'll be right down."

She closed and pocketed her cell phone, before turning to Laurel. "Lock this behind me," she said, pointing at the screen door. "And keep that gun of yours handy – but out of sight."

Laurel smiled at the detective and shifted her weight a bit, causing the butt of the 9mm to brush against her spine under the oversized tee shirt she was wearing. She watched Det. Murdoch stride down the sandy path to the beach, thinking bed head looked good on her.

Locking the screen door and then the sliding glass doors, Laurel grabbed Tut and headed upstairs to her chair on the balcony, knowing she'd have a much better view from there.

Using the night vision binoculars, she watched the police milling about taking notes, as they tried to gather all the evidence, from the crime scene before the tide washed it all away. Even without the night vision binoculars, picking Det. Murdoch out of the group of men was easy, she was the one giving orders.

Knowing that it was going to be a while before the detective would return to question her, she placed her gun on the side table, and sat back to watch the silent movie playing out on the beach.

Long before the arrival of the County Coroner the deputies were forced to move the body or risk losing it to the sea.

Once the Coroner arrived, the body was loaded, and the Coroner's vehicle left the beach. At that point Laurel knew the detective would soon be coming to question her. She returned her gun to its spine holster and quietly closed the bedroom door behind her so as not to wake a sleeping Tut.

Downstairs she made a pot of coffee, poured it into a thermos and started a second pot. She cocked her head to listen for any evidence that Tut was awake. Experience told her that an unhappy kitty could be quite destructive and Tut didn't appreciate being closed up in a room by himself.

I just don't need him deciding to tear something up. Better unhappy than escaped and roaming the streets though.

With Det. Murdoch and possibly others coming up from the beach to interview her, she didn't need Tut deciding to slip out an open door.

Her mind flashed back to the accusations from Rachel's family. That somehow, she had caused Rachel's death, so she could have all the lottery winnings and Rachel's life insurance too.

Stupid, greedy people! I would give it all back if I could have Rachel back.

The last time Laurel saw any of Rachel's family was at the reading of the will. From her half of the lottery winnings, Rachel had given each of her closest blood relatives $10,000.00. If they contested the will and lost, they would each get only $100.00.

Laurel heard the squeak of shoes in soft sand before she saw, Det. Murdoch and Deputy Brighton coming up the sandy path from the beach.

Her mind pulled up her previous experience of being a murder suspect, sitting in an interrogation room for hours.

How naïve I was to think that simply because I was innocent, I didn't need a lawyer. A lesson learned, and I won't be left sitting in some drab, cold room for hours this time.

Laurel welcomed the detective and the deputy. She gave each a cup of coffee without asking if they wanted one.

She gave a detailed statement of what she'd seen and answered all their questions. As the two law enforcement officers were leaving, Murdoch stopped at the front door and said, "I'll have this typed up as a formal statement, I'll need you to come to the office and sign it." She paused. "I'd also like you to sit with a sketch artist and see if we can get an idea of what these two women look like."

"No problem."

Before Laurel closed the door, Murdoch turned and asked, "By the way, did you get that lawyer?"

Without a word Laurel produced Mr. Davis' card and handed it to Murdoch, who glanced at the card, before tucking it in a pocket. "Thanks."

Why did she ask me a question she already knew the answer to? Mr. Davis said that he would let her know he was my attorney. I suppose it's possible Mr. Davis hadn't gotten around to calling the detective yet but somehow, I think it's just the detective playing mind games with me.

Laurel smiled and thought about other games that would be much more fun to play with the detective.

What the hell is wrong with me? Rachel's only been – gone… How long has it been now? She sighed. *Eighteen months and five days. That's how long. Still, why does she have to be a cop?*

CHAPTER 14

The sun was just coming up when I opened the bedroom door to release Tut from captivity. Instead of running from the room, he lay on the bed barely lifting his head to acknowledge my presence. He gave me a look that said, "I really don't care if the door is open or closed but you will pay for leaving me in here alone all this time."

Rubbing the top of the V-shaped head I said, "Yes, I know you're pissed about being left in here, but you sir are a real Houdini and I have no intention of letting you escape." I picked him up and cradled him in my arms as I headed to the kitchen. It was past breakfast time for both of us.

After breakfast I opened my laptop and searched the internet for software used to create people's faces. I had no desire to sit in some fluorescent lit office trying to describe the women from last night to a frustrated artist.

It didn't take me long to find a free program, download it, and start using it to create the faces of the two women I'd seen the previous night. In less than an hour, I had created both faces to the best of my memory. I printed them out and studied them for a moment. Satisfied that these were the women from the previous night, I went upstairs to shower and dress.

A polo shirt, a pair of shorts, and my walking shoes with short socks had become my uniform for life here at the beach. Although I didn't look forward to visiting the local Sheriff's department sub-station, I did want to get out of the house for a while.

As a reward for being a good boy, I sprinkled a high-quality catnip on a large brown paper bag and watched the sleek black cat as he charged into the bag, and raced in and out of it, pushing it around the room. While he played with his catnip covered bag, I talked to him. "You know I'm not sure what's going on around here but I'm beginning to think we should sell this place and move somewhere with less dead bodies lying around." I looked down to see the panther like cat with his body, low to the floor, his hind quarters wiggling, as he prepared to charge into the bag once more. Smiling at the antics of my feline friend I finished another cup of coffee.

In the end, he pounced on the bag, flattening it, grabbing the bottom fold, and kicking it for all he was worth. Exhausted from his efforts Tut crashed into a sound sleep on top of his bag. I knew he would be out for several hours. Without his antics or even his presence following me around the house and jumping into my lap, the house was too quiet.

I reached down and rubbed the ears of the miniature sleeping panther. "I'll be gone for a little while, not that you'll notice, sleepy head."

As I got into my vehicle, I placed the print outs of the two women's faces in the passenger seat. I pushed the button to raise the garage door and was greeted by two people standing in my driveway.

The man had a large camera on his shoulder, the woman held a microphone. At first, I thought they were going to rush into the garage but instead they hovered just outside the entrance. I turned the printouts face down and got out of the car.

"What do you people want?" I addressed the woman with the microphone.

The young woman signaled her cameraman, then turned to me. "What can you tell us about the murder on the beach last night?"

I knew I had to answer the police honestly; however, these people weren't the police and I had zero qualms about lying to them.

"Murder?" I hoped my expression showed the same horror as I tried to put into my voice. My hair had gone grey at an early age giving me the appearance of being older than I really was and I never hesitated to play the age card if I thought it would benefit me. I made certain to allow my voice to shake a bit. It added to the impression of me being much older than my years. "Is that what all that noise on the beach was about in the wee hours?" My hand to my heart I continued, "I woke up and looked down from my balcony, when I saw it was the local authorities and not some party going on" I shrugged "I put ear plugs in and went back to bed."

The newswoman ran a finger across her throat and the cameraman pushed a button to stop recording. I saw the red light on the camera go out and watched him lower the device to the ground as his female companion handed him the microphone. I stepped closer to the woman and quietly said, "Now, get off my property before I call the police, and have you arrested for trespassing." My voice was strong and firm. It no longer quavered.

The young woman looked at me in surprise. A slow smile turned up her bright red lips, a smile that said she understood I had seen everything last night, but I wasn't going to share that information with the public. "Round One goes to the lady with the beach house."

My tone was full of innocence, and my voice once again implied old age. "I don't understand what you mean, young lady."

The newswoman and her cameraman walked down the street to their van. I backed my car out of the garage, put the door down, and waited for the news van to leave before I pulled onto the street.

I put the address that was on Detective Murdoch's business card into my navigation system. Since Coventry Beach was a small town it didn't take long to get anywhere and the sub-station for the County Sheriff's Department was no exception.

A couple of miles inland in an industrial / office park the end unit bore the Sheriff's Department sign. There was definitely no problem finding a parking space. Sitting in the car staring at the front door with the gold badge painted on it I was reminded of the time I'd spent inside a police station answering endless questions about Rachel's death.

Damn it! I hate Police Stations and Hospitals. Both remind me of Rachel's death. I took a deep breath and got out of the car, with the printouts in hand.

Even though this was a sub-station in a small town, it had all the security measures I remembered from the big city police station. The bulletproof glass at the front desk was clean and so was the desk of the young woman sitting behind it.

"Good morning, ma'am. How may I help you?" Her soft southern drawl and warm smiling face were intended to be welcoming, although her drawl sounded a bit put on to my ears. It was as if she was trying to fit in and doing a poor job of it.

"Good morning." A study of her uniform gave me her name and the fact that she wasn't a full-fledged deputy. She was a cadet.

I suppose that's another cost cutter. Have the cadets work the front desk at a sub-station as part of their training.

"I'm here to see Detective Murdoch."

"Your name?" The fake southern drawl was still there but the attempt at warmth was gone.

I was quite certain that the iciness of her tone had been brought about by the mention of Det. Murdoch's name. I made a point of noting this for future reference. Why doesn't she like Murdoch? Because she's a lesbian? Because she's made a pass at her? No, maybe because she hasn't made a pass at her.

She repeated the question. "Your name?"

My voice showed no emotion as I answered, "Laurel Carpenito."

The disapproving look that crossed her face was there and gone so fast, I wasn't sure I had seen it at all. Without a word she picked up the phone, punched in a couple of numbers, and soon said, "Laurel Carpenito is here." After her statement she immediately hung up the phone.

In less than thirty seconds, the door next to Cadet Donner's desk opened and Det. Murdoch greeted me.

"Good morning, Ms. Carpenito." She led me through the doorway and down a corridor. "I have your statement ready. All you need to do is read it and if it's accurate, sign it."

At the end of the corridor, I followed the detective into a small office that was furnished with a typical government issue, gray metal desk on top of which sat a laptop and a couple of file folders. Det. Murdoch moved behind the desk as she offered me the chair in front of it. "Like I said, I've got your statement ready; however, I can't get a sketch artist to this side of the county for a couple of days." She smiled. "With the budget cuts we've been having we share a sketch artist with two other counties."

She picked a folder from her desk. "However, I do have a couple of photographs I'd like you to look at." Murdoch passed two eight by tens across her desk.

I took the photos and as I studied the grainy images, I could feel Murdoch watching me – watching to see what reaction I would have to the pictures. Taking my time, I looked from one image to the other, before looking up, and handing the photos back to Murdoch. "I can't say I recognize either of these men. I take it they're the ones that robbed the turtle nest."

"Yes, and most likely the ones who killed Natalie Kramer." She put the photos back in the folder and then looking straight at me asked, "You're sure you don't recognize either of them."

Without hesitating or looking away, I responded, "Positive. They're not my type." I continued to hold her gaze and was determined not to be the one to break the silence. The ball was in her court.

I continued to sit on the edge of the chair, having decided that getting physically comfortable in the detective's presence wasn't a good idea. Relaxing physically could lead to letting down my mental guard, something I had no intention of doing with the detective.

She broke eye contact and opened a desk drawer from which she pulled another file folder. "As I said earlier, I have your statement ready. I'll need you to read it, make any necessary changes, and sign it. I'll let you know when I can schedule the sketch artist."

"It's just as well that you weren't able to get the sketch artist. I really wasn't looking forward to spending my time describing people to him – or her."

"Yes, but that doesn't help me find these women." Det. Murdoch kept her tone level, reflecting no disappointment or judgment on me for not wanting to sit with a sketch artist.

"Perhaps these will help with that." I passed the printouts across the desk. "You can look those over while I read the statement you prepared."

She reached across the desk and took the papers from me. Her eyes moved quickly from one paper to the next and back to me. I was unable to prevent a smile from spreading across my face. The confused look on the detective's face was just the reaction I'd been after.

Pleased with myself, I scooted back in the chair, just a bit. "You can see in the corner the name of the software used to create the images. The software is free. Just download and go to town." My arms rested on the arms of the chair and it occurred to me that there may have been times when the person sitting in that chair had been handcuffed to it. I glanced down at my arms and felt a slight tingle at the idea of being handcuffed by Det. Murdoch. I pushed the thought away, returned to the edge of the chair, and cleared my throat. "The sour looking one" Murdoch turned one of the images toward me "yes, that one. She's the one that stabbed the man. The other one just watched."

Murdoch dropped the printouts to her desk, studied them a moment, stood up, and looked at me. "I've used night vision and there's no way you can see this kind of detail." Leaning forward, with her fists on her desk, she asked, "So do you want to tell me how you really saw this kind of detail? Or is this simply your idea of fun, giving the local yokels pictures of imaginary killers? Sending us off on a wild goose chase." She straightened up. "You know, Ms. Carpenito before you showed up here there hadn't been a murder in this town in over a year. Now we've had two in less than a week."

I stood up and in a very controlled voice said, "May I read the statement you prepared for me to sign?" This wasn't going the way I planned at all. I was hoping that the detective and I could at least become friends.

Murdoch handed me the document from the file folder on her desk. "You know if you sign that and any part of it's false, you can be arrested on a variety of charges, ranging from lying to a law enforcement officer to obstructing an investigation."

61

I read the statement, pulled a pen from my pocket, signed the document, and handed it back to Murdoch. "Good luck proving any part of that statement to be false."

CHAPTER 15

Back at her desk, after escorting Laurel out of the station, Murdoch looked over the signed statement. She examined the signature, which was little more than a collection of squiggly lines and sighed.

With that scrawl there's no way I can tell what name she signed. It could be her real name. It could be her assumed name. Damn it! I need to find a way to either prove she's tied to these murders or not. Either way, I don't think she's stupid enough to sign a false statement.

She dropped the signed statement into her desk drawer along with the printouts Laurel had delivered.

It had been a long time since Murdoch used any night vision device, so she figured maybe, just maybe the quality of imaging had been improved.

Maybe Laurel Carpentino really did see the women in the sketches.

After some intense research, Murdoch realized she had been wrong.

I suppose I owe Laurel Carpenito or Larissa Carpenter, whatever it is she wants to call herself an apology. Night vision binoculars have come a long way since I last used them. Besides, I doubt the ones the department uses are as high end as what she's using. Not with the budget cuts going on.

She put the signed statement in the case file, grabbed the two sketches, and headed to the copy machine.

With a stack of copies of each of the sketches she stopped at the front desk and left a stack of a few of the copies there. "Cadet Donner make sure that patrol deputies get a copy of each of these sketches. Thanks." And she was out the door.

The drive to the main Sheriff's Department office took Murdoch about thirty minutes. During that time, she wondered what it would be like to have virtually unlimited funds. Not what it would be like for the Sheriff's Department, but what would it be like for an individual to never have to worry about having enough money.

Murdoch went directly to the shift Sergeant's office and said, "Can you make sure every patrol car gets at least two of each of these? And that they're used to put out a statewide BOLO?"

He looked at the images and then up at Murdoch.

Before he could say anything, she said, "Those are from our eyewitness to last night's beach stabbing."

"I thought you weren't able to get a sketch artist."

Murdoch smiled. "I wasn't. Didn't need to. Check out the bottom right corner. Gotta go." Yeah, I could have scanned those in and emailed them over but then I would have missed the look on his face.

And she was out the door and headed downstairs to the forensics lab. She wanted to touch base with Paul.

At the bottom of the stairs Murdoch saw her target in the hallway. "Hey Paul."

Paul Squire stopped and turned. "Are you lost detective? This isn't the coast, you know."

"Believe me I know. I had some business over here and I just wanted to stop in and personally thank you for the work on that cell phone."

Paul Squire was head of the forensics lab for the county and he wasn't used to being treated like a person. Most of the deputies and detectives treated him and his team like lab rats and were more often than not, quite demanding. They seemed to expect him and his team to produce the miracles they saw on the television shows.

Murdoch's appreciation sparked suspicion. "What do you want, Murdoch?"

A look of innocence on her face, Murdoch spread her arms, her hands palm up, and said, "Nothing. I just wanted to say thanks." She shrugged. "Now that I've done that, I'll head back to the coast." She turned and started up the stairs.

"Murdoch."

She stopped and turned back to face Paul. "Yeah."

"Thanks. We don't get much appreciation around here."

Murdoch smiled. "I can believe that. Later." And she turned to head up the stairs.

"You know the FBI is in town and interested in the Natalie Kramer case." His words stopped her.

She turned back. "Really. What else do you know?"

CHAPTER 16

I didn't know where I was going when I left Murdoch's office. I only knew I needed to get out in the world among people. I needed to not be alone.

When I pulled into the parking space at My Place, I hadn't made a conscious decision to go there. It wasn't far from my house. Rachel and I had gone there the day we decided to buy the beach house. It was a lovely tea and coffee shop. The menu included a few bakery items, nothing extraordinary. If I remembered correctly, the cake donuts were good.

It just seemed to be the place I needed to be at the moment. Sitting in the parked car, I hesitated. I hated standing in a place trying to decide what to order. So, I sat in the car for a few moments thinking about what I wanted.

A cup of tea sounds really good right now. Yes, some Lady Grey and a cake donut.

My decision made; I entered the shop. Just inside the door, I paused, and looked around. In the far corner, away from the windows, two men sat at a table. Each had his thick fingers wrapped around a steaming mug of coffee. Between them on the table was a partially eaten cinnamon bun that covered most of the plate beneath it. My eyes moved past the unmanned counter to a table by the large plate glass window.

My Place was across the street from the beach. The only things obstructing the view of the ocean were an occasional passing car and the low sand dunes. One of the three window tables was occupied by a woman drinking tea. I couldn't see her face because she was turned, looking out the window.

I heard the swinging door of the kitchen and turned toward the counter. A warm lilting voice with an accent that sounded to me like it came straight from the French Quarter of New Orleans, floated across the room. "Welcome to My Place. Is this your first visit?" asked a woman wiping her flour covered hands on her apron.

I stepped to the counter. "No, I've been here once before, but it was a couple of years ago."

"My name is Harriet Walsh and I'm the new owner. I'm happy to see returning customers." She paused. "If you don't mind me asking, why has it been so long since your last visit?"

"Nice to meet you, Harriet. I'm Laurel Carpenito." I paused. "The last time I was here, we had just purchased a house on the beach, but we ended up not moving into it. Instead, it became a rental property."

Harriet seemed to relax. "Well, I'm glad to know it wasn't because of the product or service you received here."

I smiled. "No, as I remember we thoroughly enjoyed our visit."

Glancing around the room again, it dawned on me that the two men and the tea drinking woman were the only customers. I sighed and smiled at Harriet. "I hope business picks up for you."

Harriet smiled, her white teeth in sharp contrast to her dark caramel skin tone. "Me too." She sighed. "I'm sure it will. Just as soon as the police find out who's leaving all the dead bodies on the beach. What can I get for you?"

"Well, I'm not going to let a little thing like a couple of murders keep me away from a relaxing cup of tea. "

"Which tea do you prefer?"

I studied the chalk menu board on the wall behind Harriet. "Something light. I don't see Lady Grey."

67

"Lady Grey is a proprietary blend that belongs to Twining's. As a fan of Lady Grey, I'm sure you'll find Lady Anna to be quite enjoyable."

"I'll give her a try then."

"Excellent. Anything to go with it?"

"Yes, a cake donut."

Harriet's smile vanished. "Really?" she asked in disbelief, as if everyone knew you didn't eat a cake donut with Lady Anna tea.

She clapped her hand over her mouth and despite her dark complexion I could tell she was blushing. "I'm sorry. I can't believe I said that out loud. It's just..." she waved her hands in the air as if trying to erase her words. "No, never mind. I'm really sorry." She took a deep breath and moving toward the cash register said, "Lady Anna. Did you want a cup or a pot?"

"A pot." I was on the verge of laughing. Obviously, Harriet thought that a cake donut with Lady Anna tea was sacrilege. "Instead of a cake donut, what would you recommend?"

Harriet pulled her lower lip into her mouth and hesitated briefly, before saying, "Madeleines would be a perfect complement to Lady Anna."

"Then Madeleines it shall be." I paid for my order and chose the window table farthest from the other woman's table. Staring out the window, I tried to concentrate on the scenery, but the reality was that a spaceship could have landed in front of me and I wouldn't have noticed it. My mind was elsewhere, as I tried to piece together the events of the past few days. When Harriet brought my tea and Madeleines, I jumped.

"I'm so sorry I didn't mean to startle you."

I found Harriet's warm accent comforting and while Tut was great company he wasn't much of a conversationalist.

"No, I'm sorry here I am with all these lovely aromas and this beautiful view and I'm... Well, let's just say I'm not in the here and now."

Harriet smiled. "Enjoy your tea. Let me know what you think of the Madeleines. If you don't like them, I'll refund your money." She started back to her kitchen.

"Won't you sit with me for a moment?" I looked at the little shell shaped cakes. "They look delicious and smell wonderful."

Harriet looked around at the nearly empty room and sighed before taking the chair opposite me. "I'd be delighted."

Once she was seated, I said, "Now tell me why Madeleines are the perfect choice to go with Lady Anna."

She blushed again. With gently arched jet-black eyebrows over warm brown eyes, high cheek bones, full lips, and a strong jawline, I noted Harriet was a handsome woman. Not what some would consider pretty but good looking, none the less. Her hair was pulled back in a hairnet, giving her features a more severe look than if it were down, framing her face.

I gave a small laugh and picked up the tea pot to pour. "Don't be embarrassed. You know your products and what goes with what the best. However, instead of getting offended when someone orders a combination that you don't think is the best. Try something like..." I set the beautifully decorated tea pot down, slipped the thermal padded cozy back over it, and held Harriet's gaze. "Tell you what, you pretend to order some Lady Anna and I'll pretend to be you."

It was obvious that Harriet was hesitant to play along with me.

"Come on, I promise it won't hurt."

She smiled. "Okay." She cleared her throat. "I'd like a pot of Lady Anna."

"Excellent choice. Would you like some Madeleines to go with that? They're the perfect companion for that tea." I shrugged. "If the person still wants to order their cake donut, let them. Not everyone will be willing to experiment and try new things. Even if the expert right in front of them tells them the best choice."

Her face lit up and she said, "Thank you. I'll work on that." She looked around the cafe. "I'm not much of a people person or a salesperson. I'm a baker and I know tea and coffee." She again looked around at the near empty café. "But I'm beginning to wonder if this was the right investment."

I sipped the tea. "Hmmmm. Yes, you definitely know tea. This is even better than I expected." I gave a contented sigh, then nibbled one of the Madeleines. I closed my eyes and savored the soft, moist, buttery cake with a hint of lemon. I swallowed and opened my eyes. "If you ever decide to stop baking, please, give me the recipe for these. And you were right, these are much better than a cake donut."

A slight laugh in her voice, Harriet stood and said, "I make a wicked cake donut and it's perfect with coffee. It's just not the best choice to go with Lady Anna."

I took another bite of the heavenly cake. "You should put this combo on the menu board. Call it the Two Ladies."

Harriet left me to enjoy my tea and Madeleines. I stared out the window looking at the sunny blue sky with wisps of clouds and the white sand of the dunes with the sea oats gently swaying in the light breeze.

I don't know anyone in this town, which has its advantages as well as disadvantages. I take that back I do know a couple of people. The problem is that one is a detective who thinks I came to town to up the murder statistics and the other is a criminal defense attorney.

"Excuse me." The woman from the other window table was standing next to my table. "Larissa? Larissa Carpenter? Is it really you?"

I blinked and stared at the woman standing next to my table. It took me a moment to recognize Amber Hoffner, high school was a long time ago. The dark brown hair was still luxurious and long, her eyes were still a cornflower blue, but it was obvious life had taken a bit of their sparkle, and her smile didn't quite reach her eyes. Her smooth white skin didn't show any sign of scars but there was something about her that told me life had not been particularly kind to her.

"Amber? What in the world…" I stood up and stepped into a brief embrace, then motioned for her to have a seat. "I was just sitting here thinking about how I don't know anybody in this town and here you are. Do you live here?"

"No, but we're thinking about moving here."

"We?" I looked around the room.

"Brian's back at the hotel. He wanted to sleep in." Amber stared out the window. "It really is lovely here."

"Yes, it is."

There was an awkward pause that I broke with, "So tell me what you've been doing since high school."

I only listened with half an ear as Amber droned on about her work in computer programming, at least I think that was what she was describing.

"…About two months ago I met Brian, and well, he's…" She paused, blushing lightly. "…well, he's just fantastic." She giggled, which somehow seemed out of character for her. "I believe I've found my soul mate."

I was lost in my own thoughts and it took me a moment to realize I should have had some kind of reaction to whatever it was that

Amber had said. I apologized. "I'm sorry." I paused and took a deep breath. "I've just had a couple of rough…" I was going to say days. But then it struck me that it was more like months, and not just a couple. Ever since Rachel had died, my life had been a jumbled mess of emotions.

Joy at having won the state's largest lottery jackpot in its history. Devastating sorrow at the loss of Rachel. And now, well now, I wasn't even sure what I was feeling other than being concerned about two murders happening within sight of my house and being a murder suspect.

I looked at Amber and a wave of suspicion washed over me. Why has she suddenly appeared in my life? Yes, we knew each other in high school. We were lab partners in chemistry. We didn't run with the same crowd. Who am I kidding? I didn't run with any crowd. I was the quintessential loner.

"I'm sorry, Amber. I need to go." I stood and was several steps from the table when I returned and leaning close to Amber said, "I go by Laurel Carpenito, now. Got it? Laurel Carpenito." Before she could form a response, I was out the door and in my car.

*   *   *   *

Laurel's car was out of sight by the time Brian entered the tea shop. Amber watched him as he walked from the door to her table. He was barely seated when she began, "I'm sorry Brian. I don't know what spooked her."

"Don't worry about it." He assured her.

Harriet came out of the kitchen and started toward their table, Brian waved her off and stood up. "Let's go."

CHAPTER 17

To say I wasn't pleased to find that there were news vans parked in my driveway and up and down my street was a huge understatement. On top of that, there was a mess of cars parked in the vacant lot next to the house.

I slowed down and looked over the crowds of media. Susie Conklin pointed at my vehicle and directed her cameraman toward it. Even though I knew they couldn't see me through the tinted windows, I found it disturbing that she recognized my vehicle.

Rather than face the media and Looky Lous that surrounded my house, I turned down the first cross street I came to, Seashell Drive. I drove far enough down the street to be out of sight of my house and called Detective Murdoch.

"Hello Ms. Carpenito."

"They have my house surrounded." I knew my agitation showed in my voice.

I could hear her smile. "What ever happened to the polite pleasantries? Things like, hello Detective Murdoch. How are you this afternoon?"

Realizing I had been a bit rude, I took a deep breath and started again. "Hello Detective Murdoch. How are you this afternoon?"

"Just another day in paradise. What can I do for you, Ms. Carpenito?"

I stifled the impulse to yell that she could get rid of the hordes of news people and tourists that were invading my privacy. Instead, in a calm and light voice, I said, "Is there anything you can do about the paparazzi that have surrounded my home?"

"Unfortunately, unless they're actually trespassing on your property or obstructing traffic there really isn't…"

I cut her off. "They're in my driveway and there are cars parked in my lot."

"You own the vacant lot as well as the house?"

"Yes, is that a problem?"

"No ma'am. No problem at all, Ms. Carpenter."

I noticed her use of my legal name. "Okay, so you've proven that you're enough of a detective to figure out my real name. Bravo. Now are you going to help me, or should I take matters into my own hands?"

"Somehow I don't think either of us want you to 'take matters into your own hands'. I'll have Deputy Brighton stop by and clear out the riff-raff." I could still hear the smile in Murdoch's voice. "Later on, I'll stop by and discuss my options regarding help or handcuffs."

Murdoch ended the call and I stared at my phone, wondering exactly what Murdoch's last comment meant.

The house on the corner was vacant, so I walked down and positioned myself where I could see my house without being seen. Watching through binoculars I watched Deputy Brighton arrive.

I watched as he talked with the media people and walked into the vacant lot looking for the owners of the vehicles parked there. As he moved closer to the beach, I lost sight of him as the house blocked my view.

A little while later he came back into view, being trailed by a group of unhappy looking people. I couldn't hear what they were saying but it was clear from their faces and postures they weren't happy with whatever Deputy Brighton had told them. At the edge of the lot, he turned around, held up his hands, and spoke to the crowd.

The news people moved in closer so they could catch what he was saying. Those with microphones held them toward the deputy.

I waited until Susie Conklin and her cameraman were in their van before I pulled back onto the main road. I drove past my house and headed back to My Place. Sitting in the parking lot I used my cell phone to search for a Toyota dealership. While there was one in town, I didn't want to use one that close to home. After locating one that was 80 miles west, I went inside My Place.

Harriet came out of the kitchen at the sound of the door chime. Smiling she said, "Happy to see you again, Laurel." She reached under the counter and produced a white paper bag. "I bagged the Madeleines you left in case you came back for them."

I blushed, remembering how I had bolted from the café earlier. "Thanks. I just well, I was just feeling a little…"

Harriet laughed and said, "You don't owe me an explanation, chère." She shrugged. "Sometimes we just need to get away from whatever." She paused and changed the subject. "What can I get for you?"

Happy for the topic shift I smiled. "I need a large black coffee, a cake donut, and some of that Lady Anna so I can make it at home."

"I only sell loose leaf teas. Do you have the proper tea making equipment at home?"

"I don't suppose you consider hot water from a Keurig 'proper tea making equipment'." The look of horror on Harriet's face broadened the smile on my face.

I purchased a kettle for the stove, a lovely ceramic tea pot, a cozy for the tea pot, and all the other necessities to brew and serve a proper cup of tea at home. Harriet wrote out instructions on the correct way to brew either a cup or a pot of tea.

Looking at my pile of purchases I realized that I didn't want to haul them to the car dealer with me. "Can you keep all this here? I'll come by later or tomorrow at the latest, to pick it up. I'm headed out of town right now and I really don't want to take all this with me."

"No problem, chère."

CHAPTER 18

Nibbling at my donut and sipping my coffee, I headed west.

The Southern Breeze Toyota dealership looked like every other car lot I had ever been on. There were rows and rows of cars. The showroom was bright, immaculate, and large, with cubicles for salespeople here and there.

Since it was in the mid-90s with 100% humidity outside, all the salespeople were inside, unless they were out on the grounds showing a car to someone. I entered the building and moved directly to the reception desk. The teenager working there looked up from her phone, smiled and said, "Welcome to Southern Breeze. My name is Jane. How may I help you?"

I smiled in return and said, "Hello Jane. I want to talk to your best female salesperson."

The young lady blinked a couple of times and looked at something on the desk in front of her. "That would be Tammy Lopez. Let me see if she's back from lunch."

Seconds later Jane put down the phone receiver and said, "Tammy will be right out."

"Thank you. I'll be wandering around the showroom." I stepped away from the desk and ran my eyes over the various cars on the showroom floor. My attention was grabbed by a vibrant blue Prius at the far end of the room.

Circling the blue Prius, I stopped at the window sticker that listed the features and the price. Then I moved to the driver's door. It was unlocked and I sat down in the driver's seat and took a deep breath of the new car smell.

A female voice with a soft British accent asked, "Would you like to take her for a test drive?"

I looked at the time and thought about how long I'd left Tut home alone and how long it was going to take me to get back to Coventry Beach. "No, but I do want to buy it." I got out of the car. "How long will it take to have it ready to leave?"

The woman's smile showed large very white teeth. "That will depend on how long it takes to get the financing and…"

"No financing. I'll call my bank and have the funds wired to the dealership's account for the sale of the car and whatever the commission is will be wired directly to an account of your choosing." I took a breath. "I'll pay the sticker price but there will be no tax, tag, or title added on. The price on the window sticker. Not a penny more and not a penny less."

Tilting her head, a look of disbelief on her face, The woman said, "It usually takes the detail boys about an hour to get a car ready."

I checked the time on my phone. "If they can have it ready in thirty minutes, we have a deal. Otherwise, I'll take my business elsewhere."

"Then let's not waste another minute. Follow me." As we passed the reception desk, she said, "Jane, have the boys get that blue Prius ready to go. Tell them it's for me and they've got 25 minutes."

The woman didn't wait for a response as she continued to an office at the other end of the showroom.

"Please, have a seat…I just realized we haven't been introduced." She extended her hand. "I'm Tammy."

I shook her hand. "I'm LC."

"Nice to meet you, LC."

78

Five minutes later, my bank transferred the funds to the account numbers Tammy provided. While I talked to my banker Tammy pulled together all the requisite paperwork.

Months after winning the lottery jackpot, my attorney recommended that I change all my legal signatures to L. Carpenter and to make the 'Carpenter' as illegible as possible. Between the notoriety of winning the lottery and Rachel's subsequent death, I was constantly being peppered with requests for money and then there were the death threats, not all of which came from Rachel's family.

While we waited for the car to be prepped, Tammy asked, "So what does LC stand for?" She squinted at my signature on the sales papers.

"I love your British accent. How did you end up in Florida?"

She smiled and said, "Decisive, wealthy, and secretive. I'm intrigued. Are you married?"

"Widowed."

"Oh, I'm sorry."

I shrugged.

After a few seconds Tammy said, "Most people want to test drive a car before they buy it or at least hear the engine."

"I'm not most people."

"That becomes more and more evident with each passing second." She leaned forward in the desk chair, placed her arms on the desk and said, "Who are you LC?"

"The woman who just made your day with what was probably the easiest sale of your life."

Smiling she glanced over my shoulder, looking through the doorway of her office. "I believe Bobby has your car ready." She stood up and said, "That is true; I've never made an easier sale. Let me take you out to dinner as a thank you."

I stood up and said, "Thank you, but I have to get back to Coventry Beach."

A young man in shorts and a t-shirt stepped into the office and handed Tammy a set of car keys. "Thank you, Bobby. I'll make sure you and the boys get your usual bonus."

The well-tanned face split in a smile and with a nod to me he turned and left.

She held the keys in her hand. "I'm grateful for the sale but I have to ask, didn't you know there's a Toyota dealership in Coventry Beach."

My only response was to smile.

Handing the keys to me, she said, "Well then, let's get you on your way back to the coast."

We stepped from the air-conditioned building into the sweltering sauna that is Florida in the summer.

We walked to the car in silence. Standing in the open driver's doorway of the car, I said, "By the way, the large white SUV over there." I pointed to where I'd parked upon arrival. "The car rental people will be by to pick it up before you close tonight." I got into the car and put on my seatbelt as I familiarized myself with the dashboard.

Tammy tapped on the window and I lowered it. "I'll check in with you in a few days to see how things are going."

I smiled. "Feel free but there's no need. Electra and I will be getting along just fine."

"Electra?"

"Yes." I looked at her questioningly. "I name all my cars. Don't you?" Not giving her time to respond, I put the window up, backed out the parking space and headed for the exit.

CHAPTER 19

As I cruised east on Interstate 4, I could see the rain clouds ahead.

The thunder I heard seemed to be trying to match the unhappy sounds from my stomach, which was growling. It dawned on me that since breakfast all I'd eaten was one small Madeleine and a single cake donut.

Talking out loud I said, "I suppose I should stop somewhere for something to eat. But I really want to get home to Tut. I know I'll go to My Place, get my tea stuff and see if Harriet has any Spanakopita left."

By the time I pulled into the parking lot at My Place the rain was a typical Florida summer rain. The large drops were accompanied by flashes of lightning and blasts of thunder.

I dashed for the door and was quickly inside. The aromas of coffee, tea, and fresh baked bread only increased my hunger. I stopped and inhaled deeply of the delightful smells.

Harriet stood at the counter watching me. I was in an exceptionally good mood. I approached the counter saying, "Harriet, if you were a lesbian, I'd marry you, just so I could have you cook for me all the time."

Deep laughter rumbled out of her and her teeth flashed in a warm smile. "Chère, you can come here every day and have me cook for you. No need for all that marriage nonsense." She nodded toward the parking lot. "That where you went, to get a new car?"

"Yeah. The SUV was a rental and the news lady, Susie Conklin got where she knew it, so I figured I'd get myself a new car. Though

I doubt it will take her long to figure out my new set of wheels." I grinned. "Want to go for a joy ride?"

"Some other time, Chère. I'm running a business here, you know. What can I get for you?"

"I'm starving and I need to get home. Do you have any Spanakopita left and can I get it to go? Oh yeah, and I'll go ahead and take my tea making supplies with me."

A few minutes later Harriet returned from the kitchen and handed me a bag. "If you eat it as soon as you get home, you shouldn't need to heat it. If you let it get cold, you'll need to put it in the oven at 350 for about 10 to 15 minutes."

CHAPTER 20

On the early evening news, I heard what Deputy Brighton had said to the crowd. "This vacant lot is private property. You are all trespassing. The landowner will be posting the property and plans to prosecute all trespassers. Everyone needs to vacate this lot immediately."

Well, I guess that means I'll have to find out where to get the appropriate signage.

The camera followed him as he turned to go back to his patrol car. He stopped next to his vehicle and pointing at the vehicles in my driveway, he added, "Those vehicles also need to go."

The same newswoman, Susie Conklin, that I'd dealt with earlier that day, spoke as the video showed the people removing their cars from the lot and my driveway. "The deputy went on to tell everyone present that street parking was limited and he would be back in fifteen minutes to verify that all remaining vehicles were legally parked and that no one was trespassing on private property." She took a breath. "In other news…"

I turned off the television and rubbed Tut's ears. "Don't worry old man. They'll find some other newsworthy story soon enough and then they'll forget all about us."

I hope.

A clap of thunder shook the house, I smiled as Tut stretched. The storm outside didn't seem to have any effect on him. He nuzzled my hand, requesting more ear rubs. Rubbing the cat's ears, I began to drift off to the sound of purring and the pitter patter of windblown rain on the windows. Dead bodies, the media, and the sudden appearance in my life of Amber Hoffner had proven exhausting.

The jarring sound of the doorbell made me jump, waking Tut. I lowered the leg rest of the recliner and placed the cat on the seat of the chair as I got up to see who was at the door.

Looking through the peephole I saw Amber, a rather wet Amber. The wind was driving the rain sideways and outside my front door offered zero protection from the weather.

The lack of protection at the front door from the weather was one of the few imperfections that Rachel and I discussed before buying the house. We decided it was something that would be easy to fix but then…

Despite being annoyed at the interruption of my nap I didn't feel right about leaving Amber standing in the rain, so I opened the door and wordlessly invited the dripping woman into the house.

It hadn't been that long ago that I'd been caught in an unanticipated rain shower while out walking the neighborhood. Since then, I kept a towel in the coat closet by the front door. I reached into the closet and presented Amber with the towel.

"How did you find me?" Not giving Amber time to respond I continued, "Or perhaps the better question is, why are you here?"

Amber accepted the towel and dried her shoulder length brown hair. Her clothes were plastered to her body and she shivered.

I kept the house at seventy-six degrees, which was quite comfortable unless of course you were standing under an air vent in wet clothes.

Tut meowed and looked with displeasure upon the new arrival. I glanced at him as if to say, "Well, what did you expect me to do? Leave her standing outside in the rain?"

The cat's response was to pull his tail up over his nose and go back to sleep.

I turned back to the shivering Amber, pointed to the bathroom, and said, "Go in there and get out of those wet things. There's a robe hanging on the back of the door. Put it on and bring me your clothes."

Amber's wet flip-flops smacked across the tile floors as she followed my instructions. Minutes later she emerged from the bathroom wearing the white Terri cloth robe that was at least a size too big for her slight body. Her wet clothes were bundled in the towel, which she handed to me.

I took the wet bundle and pointing to the breakfast bar that separated the kitchen and the living room, said, "Have a seat."

As Amber moved toward the bar, I stepped into the laundry room, dumped the wet bundle into the dryer, and turned it on. Closing the door to the laundry room I said, "By the time the storm is over everything should be dry."

On the bar in front of Amber's seat was a steaming mug. I pointed at it. "Hot chocolate. It'll take the chill off."

"Thank you." She wrapped her hands around the ceramic mug. "It's amazing how you can go from being so hot you feel like you're going to melt to shivering."

I studied Amber sipping her hot chocolate. The battles of life were more visible on her face now with her hair pulled back in a ponytail. "You were just foolish enough to get soaking wet and enter an air-conditioned building."

A look of anger, annoyance, irritation, or something else crossed Amber's face but was gone in a flash.

"Sorry, I've never been particularly good at the social niceties. And now with everything that's happened lately, I'm even less inclined to be hospitable."

Amber removed her hands from the mug and pulled the robe closer to her. "Well, I was concerned about you. The way you tore out of the tea shop... I just wanted to make sure you were okay." Before I could respond, she quickly continued, "Then by the time I got here it was pouring. I sat in the car for a bit, but it didn't look like it was going to stop anytime soon, so I ran to the door. I didn't realize there was no protection from the rain at your front door. I figured I'd get a little damp between the car and the door. I didn't count on getting soaked."

I held her gaze and considered how I wanted to respond. I mean I already told her I wasn't feeling particularly hospitable.

"Two questions still remain unanswered. One, how did you find me? It's not like you could go to a phone book and look me up."

Amber waved away the idea of something as old-fashioned as a phone book. "Please, with the internet finding people is child's play. Much easier than it was in the day of phone books."

I sighed. "Yes, I suppose you're right about that. Two, why did you go to the trouble of finding me?" Amber started to speak but I cut her off. "And don't give me that bullshit story about being concerned about me. We were lab partners in high school chemistry. We were not friends. We weren't even acquaintances. So, the truth. Why?"

Amber sipped her drink. I felt like she was stalling while she tried to figure out a new story about why she came looking for me. Her eyes were focused beyond me. She was looking out the large window in the kitchen. I couldn't blame her for that. It was an entrancing sight to watch the ocean in a rainstorm.

"The truth" she said quietly. She took a deep breath and brought her eyes back to me. "The truth is that I probably should have been your friend in high school, but I was young, and status was important. Being friends with the class lesbian wasn't good for

86

one's status." She took a sip of her drink, sat the mug on the counter, and crossed her arms. With a slight smile on her face continued. "And let's face it you piqued my interest when you told me to use the alias of Laurel Carpenito. What did you think I would do?"

She leaned forward and placed her elbows on the bar. "Just walk away?" She smiled and sat back on the stool. "Of course, all the members of my high school class are living under assumed names." Her sarcasm was unmistakable.

Her smile was replaced by an expression of concern. "What kind of trouble are you in..." she hesitated, as if she had to stop and think which name to use..."Laurel?"

I emitted a short laugh that sounded more like a bark. "You really don't know?"

"If I knew I wouldn't have asked, now would I?"

With a heavy sigh, I said, "Larissa Carpenter is one of the richest women in the country. She and...she won the state's largest lottery jackpot in history."

Eyes wide, with a stunned look on her face Amber said, "That was...I heard it was a woman named Rachel something and her partner." She swallowed audibly. "You were the partner."

At the sound of Rachel's name, I turned to the tea kettle on the stove and pretended to check it for water. Then I busied myself dumping the tea leaves from the brew basket into a compost bucket. I took a deep breath and got my emotions under control. It only took a few seconds and I reflected on that.

It used to take days, then hours, then minutes, and now I'm down to seconds.

"I get it. You got tired of everybody trying to be your friend, so they could get money from you." She paused. "When you took off the way you did, I was confused. I couldn't think of anything I'd said or done to cause your reaction. When I went back to the hotel room and told Brian what had happened. He suggested I find you and see if you were all right." She smiled. "He reminded me that if we decide to relocate here, it would be nice to start out with at least one person we knew. It seemed like a good idea at the time." She stood up. "I'll just get dressed and get out of your hair."

I still didn't one hundred percent believe Amber's story, but I wasn't willing to discount it entirely. Besides, I believe in the old saying, keep your friends close and your enemies closer. While I didn't really think Amber was an enemy, I didn't yet count her as a friend. With only Tut for company I was willing to give this relationship a chance.

"I doubt your clothes are dry yet. Drink your hot chocolate and tell me why you and Brian are thinking of moving here. It's a quiet, small town," I said out loud as I thought to myself, as long as you don't include the two recent murders. With a smile I added, "As I remember you were quite the party animal in high school or so the rumor mill said."

Amber snorted. "Yeah, that party animal thing followed me to college." Her voice carried a bitter edge to it as she continued, "A few of us ended up at the same school and the partying continued. Right up until I had an abortion." She laughed. "If you think being a lesbian makes you a pariah, let word get around that you had an abortion."

"I'm sorry." I couldn't think of anything else to say. The awkward silence that ensued was intense. I broke it with, "Let me check on your clothes."

The synthetic fabric of Amber's shorts and shirt had dried quickly.

The thunder and lightning had moved offshore, taking the driving wind with them. The rain was still falling though at a much more sedate level.

I was drying the chairs on the back screened in deck when Amber came out of the bathroom looking every inch the tourist in her flip-flops, shorts, and floral print blouse. She joined me and commented, "Oh my god, it's worse out here now than it was before the storm. Does it ever cool off around here?" She looked at me in horror.

I laughed. "Yeah, sometime around January."

Pulling the front of her blouse back and forth to create a breeze, she asked, "You're not going to sit out here, are you?"

"No, it's a bit early in the day for that." Straightening up I held the towel I'd used to wipe down the small plastic table over a bucket and wrung it out. I draped the wet towel over the back of a chair and ushered Amber back inside the house, closed, and locked the sliding glass door. Moving to the kitchen sink I emptied the bucket. "After the sun goes down, Tut and I will move out there to enjoy the ocean breeze." I sighed. "Maybe."

"Maybe?"

"I said that out loud, huh?"

Amber smiled. "Yes, you definitely said it out loud. And who is Tut?"

I motioned Amber toward the living room where she took a rocking chair across the room from the recliner, the seat of which Tut still occupied. I scooped the sleeping cat up and placed him in my lap as I sat down.

"This is Tut." I absent-mindedly stroked the top of the cat's head from the top of his nose to behind his ears where I paused to scratch, before repeating the process. "His original name was Sir

Reginald but before I learned that I'd already started calling him King Tut, Tut for short."

Tut looked up at me, stretched, repositioned himself and went back to sleep. He was still a bit groggy from his catnip high.

Petting any cat has always had a very calming effect on me. Something about having a warm furry creature in my lap is relaxing.

"So, are you going to tell me what sent you running from My Place?"

I sighed. "Let's just say I'm a bit on edge after the things that have happened around here in the past couple of days."

"The past couple of days?" She shrugged. "That's the second time you've mentioned something about stuff that's going on around here. I don't understand." She paused. "Has there been something in the news that I should know about?"

"Yes, I suppose if you're on vacation you don't pay much attention to the news." I straightened up in my chair. This conversation was having a counter effect on Tut's relaxing presence. "You may want to reconsider moving here. There have been two murders on that lovely beach out there, all within sight of this house."

Amber gasped. "Murders? Have they caught whoever did it? Is it a serial killer?"

"Yes, No, and I don't know."

"Do they have suspects?"

I laughed. "My guess is that they suspect me."

"What!?!"

"Well they have some grainy pictures of a couple of guys robbing turtle eggs and me. I doubt those pictures will do them much good. Det. Murdoch showed them to me and I don't think their own mothers would recognize those men."

The look of concern on Amber's face amused me. At the same time, I didn't want her to run out the door for fear she might be the next murder victim. "Perhaps you should call Brian and let him know that you're all right."

Amber blushed. "I would but I left my phone in the car. I didn't want it to get wet." She paused but not long enough for me to say anything. "I know they say that today's phones are fine if they get a little wet. They say you can even swim with some of them. I'm just not sure I believe it."

Tossing Amber my cell phone I said, "Here, use my phone. That is if you can remember his number."

Amber caught the phone. "Thanks. It's easy to remember his number. He paid a lot of money to get it." She read the numbers out loud as she punched them in. "202-123-4567." She put the phone to her ear and smiled. "All I really have to remember is the area code," she said while waiting for the call to connect.

Seconds later a unique and very audible ringtone was heard at the front door. It rang twice before being answered.

"Hello?"

"Hey Brian, it's me." Her voice hesitant she asked, "Where are you?"

Before he could answer, I opened the front door. Brian stood on my front doorstep with an umbrella in one hand and his cell phone in the other.

The situation was quite comical. "Hello Brian. It's nice to meet you. Why don't you hang up and step inside? You two can talk face-to-face then."

His brown eyes moved from me standing in the doorway holding Tut to his cell phone. He started to just push the end call button, but first he brought the phone back to his face and said, "Bye. I'll be right in."

He ended the call and pocketed the phone, closed, and shook the rain from his umbrella, before stepping past me into the house.

Amber returned my phone to me and performed the introductions. "...and that small black panther Laurel is holding is King Tut."

"It's nice to meet you Laurel and you too, your majesty," Brian said with a smile. He turned to Amber, slipping his arm around her waist. "I take it everything is all right."

For a moment Amber looked confused. "Oh! Yes, Laurel's just a bit spooked by the murders that have happened, nearby on the beach."

Brian pulled Amber closer. The move was a typical reaction of a man protecting his woman. It seemed to come a split second late, as if he'd had to think about how he should react to the statement about murders. Something about their relationship was off. I didn't get the madly in love with each other vibe.

"Near here?"

"Yes, both within sight of this house," I said as my phone rang with an upbeat, bouncy tune.

On the heels of my phone ringing Brian's phone gave an audible bark like sound from the pocket of his shorts.

Looking at Brian I asked, "Was that the cry a hungry juvenile White Bald Eagle?"

"Yes. Not many people recognize the sound."

I smiled and studied my phone's screen for a few seconds. It was the private investigation agency I'd hired, to investigate Amber's background since high school.

"Excuse me a moment. I should take this." I stepped away from the couple and placed Tut in the seat of the recliner. "Hello."

It was a short conversation and I ended it with, "Thank you. I appreciate your assistance. I look forward to receiving your report. Goodbye."

Disconnecting the call, I turned to my guests and said, "I imagine you two love birds have better things to do than hang around here. I suggest that you try the restaurant under the Courthouse Bridge. Whatever you order make sure you get hush puppies with it. They're the best I've ever eaten."

As I was ushering them out the door Amber asked, "Brian's not the only one with a unique ringtone. What was that ringtone on your phone?"

I smiled. "That's the theme from Miss Fisher's Murder Mysteries."

CHAPTER 21

Tut and I were enjoying an old television show, when all the security lights for the front of the house came on. Moments later the doorbell rang.

Damn! I've got to get that camera installed. This getting up just to see who's at the door is bullshit.

Looking through the peephole, I saw Susie Conklin standing there. While I was debating with myself about opening the door, "Larissa Carpenter I know you're in there. We need to talk."

Shit!

Opening the door, I motioned her to come in. I watched her as her eyes scanned the house, from the entrance to the garage, past the breakfast nook, the kitchen, the stairs, to the living room. From the recliner Tut looked at her, blinked and went back to sleep. It took her only a few seconds to take it all in.

I closed the front door. However, my hospitality was exhausted. I had no intention of inviting this distasteful woman any further into my home. We remained standing in the foyer. Truth be told I was barely civil.

"What do you want, Ms. Conklin?"

She turned to face me. "What I want is an exclusive on both the beach murders?"

"Why tell me?"

"Because you can get it for me."

I laughed. "Let's just say, hypothetically, that that's true. Why should I help you?"

Her bright red lips turned upward. "Because, if you don't tomorrow evenings news will include the fact that the state's biggest lottery jackpot winner is living in Coventry Beach under the name of Laurel Carpenito."

"Blackmail. I'm not surprised. I figured you for a low-life from the very beginning."

"No need to be nasty, Ms. Carpenter. I'm just trying to get out of this backwater town and advance my career." She paused. "This is still a predominately male business and I need to be twice as good as the men I work with just to be seen as adequate."

I needed time to decide how I was going to handle this situation. It's not like I was hiding from the law. I was simply hiding from every panhandler on the planet and Rachel's family. Yeah, Rachel's family.

"What makes you think I care if you tell the world where I am?"

"If you didn't care you wouldn't be here under an alias."

"Fair point."

"I don't care how you do it or even why you do it, as long as I get an exclusive on both beach murders." She paused. "If you assure me of that, I'll keep your real name to myself."

"Not only will you keep my name to yourself. You will keep your fellow reporters from exposing me. If you figured out who I am so will others. If I'm – outed – before the murders are resolved, I'll make certain your biggest competitor gets the exclusive."

"How do you expect me to…"

"I don't care how you do it, as long as you do it. That's the deal. Take it or leave it."

She sighed. "I'll take it."

I checked on Tut to make sure he was asleep. He had made attempts at returning to the great outdoors in the past and I had no interest in chasing him down in the middle of the night. I opened the door.

"Goodbye, Ms. Conklin."

CHAPTER 22

Despite the summer heat, Ariel Fenton shivered as she slowly moved another spade of beach sand from the hole Edith had ordered her to dig.

Edith Bates sat several feet away with a gun in one hand and a whiskey bottle in the other.

Other than Edith's small battery-operated lantern the full moon that moved in and out of the clouds was the only light to see by on this deserted stretch of beach. The park just beyond the dunes had closed at sunset and the houses on the other side of the street beyond the park were dark. Either they were unoccupied, or their residents had already gone to bed.

"Keep digging. I want to get this over with so I can go take a shower." Edith menacingly pointed the gun in Ariel's direction.

Ariel paused and leaned on the shovel handle for a moment. "I thought we were friends, Edith. Why are you doing this?"

Edith snorted a laugh. "Friends. Hah! If you were my friend, you wouldn't have slept with my husband." She planted the whiskey bottle in the wet sand next to her chair and rose on unsteady legs.

Ariel threw the shovel to the ground and with her hands on her hips said, "You're the one who asked me to test his faithfulness. You said you wanted to know if he would cheat on you."

Edith's voice was calm and cold. "Pick up the shovel and keep digging." Ariel crossed her arms and didn't move.

A wicked smile, that didn't reach her eyes, moved Edith's lips upward, as she aimed the gun at Ariel. "Pick, it, up." She enunciated each word individually. "Or…"

"Or what?" Ariel did her best to sound confident, in spite of the terror she felt. "You'll shoot me? But then who will dig the hole? What will happen to your little game of terrorizing me?"

Edith smirked as she lowered her aim from Ariel's chest and pulled the trigger. The bullet shattered Ariel's left knee and she collapsed to the sand screaming in pain. The sound of the gunshot, along with Ariel's cries were carried away by the wind.

Ignoring Ariel's screams, Edith moved the chair further away from her victim, took a swig from the whiskey bottle and placed the gun on the seat of the chair. She picked up the shovel and began the work of finishing the hole.

After a few moments, when Ariel's screams had subsided to moans, Edith looked up from her work and said, "Does this answer your question? Did you really think I would let you off with an easy death?"

Even though she was digging the hole in the hardpack of the beach, the sand was soft compared to the metal blade of the shovel and in ten minutes the hole was complete. After all Ariel was barely five feet tall. Edith straightened up, dropped the spade next to her beach chair, and took a long drink from the whiskey bottle.

Lying on the sand trying to crawl away from the hole Ariel screamed, "You're insane! You'll never get away with this. Someone must have heard that gunshot and reported it to the police."

In a few strides, Edith was in front of Ariel. She squatted down and with a maniacal grin said, "Nobody is coming to your rescue, bitch." She waved a hand at the surrounding area. "That park is closed. The houses on the other side of the road are too far away to have heard anything. Even if they did, they probably thought it was some kid playing with firecrackers."

Without further comment Edith grabbed Ariel's long black hair and began dragging her toward the hole.

Ariel regained consciousness when water slapped her in the face. She tried to reach up and wipe the salty liquid from her eyes, but her hands wouldn't move. They were pinned to her sides. Again, the water splashed her. Out of the darkness a hand brushed her hair out of her eyes, and she tried to jerk her head away.

Edith's voice soft and comforting said, "I wouldn't want you to miss seeing this." She pointed a flashlight at the ocean in front of Ariel. "You see the tide is just beginning to come in." Edith extinguished the light.

Ariel screamed in terror, but the sound was drowned out by the next incoming wave that filled her open mouth with sea water. She was buried in the sand up to her neck, facing the Atlantic Ocean and the incoming tide.

Edith sat down in her beach chair, holding her whiskey bottle, and smiling at her latest victim. "Guess you're not a mermaid after all."

In between waves Ariel pleaded, begged, and tried to reason with Edith until finally there was no, in between, and the water covered her head.

CHAPTER 23

Stretching, I looked at the digital clock on the headboard. Six-fifteen. Almost an hour before sunrise.

Well, I'm wide-awake so I might just as well get up.

Lying on his pillow Tut opened his eyes and looked at me with displeasure.

"Don't give me that look. You didn't toss and turn most of the night. You slept like the dead, while I kept waking up every couple of hours."

Wearing the boxer shorts and oversized t-shirt that I slept in I headed to the kitchen. Cancelling the timer, I started the coffee maker. While I waited for the pot to brew, I checked the water level in Tut's drinking fountain, added kibble to his dish, and placed my phone on its charging pad. Removing the fruit containers from the refrigerator I set strawberries and blue berries on a plate and separated a banana from the bunch hanging on the bar. I tossed the banana peel into the small compost bucket on the counter.

By the time I finished eating my fruit, the coffee was ready, and I poured a cup and put the remainder in a thermos.

Coffee in hand I opened the blinds to the back deck. The sight of a body on the deck's chaise lounge made me jump. Hot coffee sloshed out of my cup. Hitting the tile floor, and splashing onto my bare feet, causing me to jump again, spilling more coffee.

"Damn it!"

The body on the chaise lounge moved and I watched Carly Reddington stretch, sit up, and swing her long tan legs over the edge of the chaise.

Trying to control my anger I placed the, now half-empty coffee cup, on the bar. I peeled off several paper towels and dropped them on the coffee puddle before turning my gaze back to the chaise lounge on the deck.

Carly was now standing at the sliding glass door wearing a confused expression.

Fists on my hips, I moved toward the glass door. "Do you have any idea...what the hell are you trying to do? Give me a heart attack? It's not bad enough I've nearly tripped over a dead body on the beach, watched another person get stabbed to death, now I look out on my deck and there's a body on my chaise lounge." Barely taking a breath and certainly not giving Carly an opportunity to reply, I continued my harangue for several more seconds.

When I paused for a deep breath, Carly said something, I could see her lips moving but was unable to hear the words.

"What? I can't hear you very well."

Carly shrugged and pointed toward the door handle.

I sighed, unlocked the door, and moved to the kitchen.

Carly let herself in. "My apologies. I hadn't planned on falling asleep. I really am sorry I gave you such a scare." She bent down and using the paper towels I had deposited on the coffee puddle she wiped up most of the brown liquid. She reached over the bar and dropped the sopping wet paper towels into the sink and grabbed half-a-dozen fresh towels off the roll to finish mopping up the mess.

I topped off my own mug and placed a mug of the French Vanilla Roast on the bar for my guest. "If you don't drink it black, tough.

Cause I don't have any creamer. I suppose you could use some honey as sweetener – if you must."

Carly wrapped her hands around the steaming mug. "No. Black is fine." She held the mug under her nose and inhaled deeply. "Ahhh, the elixir of life." She took a sip and said, "Thank you."

"Why are you camped out on my deck?" I watched her face over her coffee mug as she sipped the hot liquid.

Carly set her mug down on the bar and lowered herself to one of the stools. "I woke up a couple of hours ago and I couldn't get back to sleep." She ran an index finger, absentmindedly around the rim of her coffee mug. "I wanted to talk to you about Natalie." She looked up from her examination of the mug as her finger continued to circle the ceramic rim. "What can you tell me about her visit with you?"

The whites of Carly's blue eyes were red. It was obvious she had been crying, most likely over the death of her friend. My attitude softened a bit. Grieving the loss of someone so close to you was something I could relate to.

I may have stumbled over Natalie's body, but Carly lost a childhood friend. I suppose I should cut her some slack.

"I'm sure Det. Murdoch told you what I already told her about that." I paused. "But if you really want, I can go over it again."

Carly smiled and exhaled as if she had been holding her breath. "Thank you."

Tut jumped up on the bar, meowed and pushed on Carly's chin with his head. Carly absentmindedly stroked the black feline as she listened to me recount Natalie's visit.

"…I knew she wasn't telling me the whole truth about why she was skulking about in the wee hours…" I shrugged "…but she was right I hadn't called the police. Maybe if I had, she'd still be alive. I

102

don't know." Looking at Carly, I asked, "Do you know what she was doing?"

"Not really, though I have my suspicions." Carly gave Tut one last scratch behind the ears before standing up. "Thanks for the coffee and I really am sorry I gave you such a fright."

"At least you weren't another dead body. One more of those and I'm selling this place and moving far, far away from Coventry Beach." I paused. "You said that you had an idea of what Natalie was up to."

"Yes, I did say that." Carly moved to the door. It was obvious she had no intention of sharing her thoughts on the topic.

"Was it illegal?" Carly stopped with her hand on the doorknob. "Is that why you won't tell me? You're trying to protect her reputation?"

Carly turned around but before she could speak, I continued, "Isn't it more important to find out who killed her?"

After several seconds of holding my gaze, Carly said, "What's more important is keeping anyone else from getting killed."

I nodded my head in agreement. "I agree, which is why this person needs to be stopped."

A sad smile pulled at the ends of Carly's lips. "That kind of thinking is probably what got Natalie killed."

CHAPTER 24

From the parking lot I could see Amber and Brian inside My Place. I watched them. It was obvious they were having an intense conversation. Some might even call it an argument. Brian didn't look happy and from Amber's body language she was tense. I couldn't see Harriet but knowing her she was watching the couple from the kitchen.

I knew from previous conversations with Harriet that she neither liked nor trusted Brian. She couldn't say why, other than she didn't like how he bossed Amber around.

Suddenly Amber stood up, knocking over her chair. I still couldn't hear her words, but I could tell she was angry about something. I decided that I should go inside, perhaps my presence would defuse the situation.

Brian stood up, his fists on the table he leaned forward. He was saying something to Amber when he saw me on my way in. Our eyes locked briefly. His entire demeanor changed and with a smile on his face he walked around the table, gently took Amber in an embrace. He held her for a few seconds before releasing her. He bent down and picked up her chair.

At that point I was coming through the doorway. The bell announcing a new customer brought Harriet from the kitchen.

Brian pulled Amber into another quick embrace. Then he stepped back, pulled her hands to his lips, kissed them like a gentleman of years gone by, and said, "Of course we can stay another week. You know I can work from anywhere I have an internet connection."

With a smile on her face Amber turned to me. "Hi there, we were just talking about you. We wanted to thank you for the restaurant recommendation. And you were right about the hush puppies. They were divine."

I returned her smile. "I'm glad you liked them. I'm always concerned that I'll recommend something I like and the person I recommended it to, won't like it."

"Why don't you put in your order and then join us?"

Nodding my agreement, I turned and moved to the counter.

Harriet was waiting for me. "Hi, Laurel. It's good to see you again."

"Hello, Harriet." I glanced up at the chalk menu board on the wall behind the counter and smiled. "I'll have the Two Ladies with a pot."

Harriet returned my smile. "An excellent choice." As she took my money, in a voice audible only to me, she said, "Be careful of him. There's something not right about those two."

I replied just as quietly, "Yeah, I just can't put my finger on it." In a more audible voice I said, "Great. I'll be sitting with the lovebirds."

Once I was seated, I asked, "So what are you two up to today? More house hunting?"

"We've been trying to decide where to have dinner tonight. Brian wants steak and I don't know what I want. I guess steak would be all right."

I sat with my back to the kitchen facing the window. "Well, I just had a grill delivered to the house, so why don't you come over to my place for dinner? I can grill a couple of steaks, make a salad, and bake some potatoes."

What the hell possessed me to invite them over? I'm not sure I trust either one of them. Despite the private investigator's assurances that they are what they say they are, I know they're not telling me the truth about why they're here in Coventry Beach, at least not all the truth.

Harriet's arrival with my order interrupted the conversation about who would bring what to the evening meal.

"Hey Harriet, why don't you join us tonight? You're new to the area and so are the rest of us. We could make it a get to know each other and the area party."

Harriet hesitated and I added, "If you have a significant other, feel free to bring them along."

Harriet smiled. "Cleo sits at home all day by herself and would love to get out."

"Excellent. Bring Cleo along."

A slight laugh in her voice Harriet said, "Cleo is a Belgian Malinois."

"Does Cleo like cats? And I don't mean to eat or use as a chew toy," I asked with laughter in my voice.

"I'm more worried about your cat attacking Cleo, than the other way around. My girl is very well trained, and she was raised with a cat."

I sighed. "And I too, am very well trained. The old saying about dogs having masters and cats having staff, is all too true. Despite my training, I'll put his majesty in the bedroom. If we get a chance, we'll introduce them and see how it goes." I looked at Amber and Brian. "Do either of you have cat or dog allergies?"

This question was met with a unanimous, "No."

I clapped my hands together and said, "Excellent. It's settled. Harriet since you're the only member of this party tied to a time clock, what time can we expect you at my house?"

When all was said and done it was decided that I would supply the grill, the salad, and baked potatoes. Amber and Brian would bring the steaks. Harriet would bring dessert.

CHAPTER 25

As I prepared for the evening's get together, I called Det. Murdoch, "Good afternoon, detective."

"Good afternoon, Ms. Carpenito. What can I do for you?"

"I'd like to invite you to dinner this evening. Before you say no, I've also invited the new owner of My Place, the little café down the road from my house, and a couple who are thinking about moving here. Look at it as an opportunity to get to know some of the new people in town, sort of a community relations thing."

There was a brief pause. "What can I bring?"

"What do you usually bring when you attend potluck dinner parties?"

"Deviled eggs it is. What time should I arrive?"

*   *   *   *

Murdoch waited down the street until Harriet arrived. Brian and Amber were already inside. She parked her unmarked police car across the end of the driveway. Before anyone else could leave, she would have to move her car.

Taking a deep breath of the warm, humid sea air, she rang the doorbell.

*   *   *   *

Cleo sat up from where she was lying next to Harriet's chair.

Brian and Amber exchanged looks and then Brian asked, "Are you expecting another guest?"

I smiled but said nothing as I moved into the house to answer the door. "Welcome, Detective Murdoch. Let me take that platter. I'll put it in the kitchen."

Murdoch handed me the platter and I left her to close the door. "Before we go any further, Ms. Carpenito, I owe you an apology."

"Really?"

"Yes. I did some research and learned that night vision binoculars have come a long way since I last used them." She paused. "Thank you for the sketches."

Once in the kitchen I placed the platter of deviled eggs on the counter and said, "Apology accepted and you're welcome. What can I get you to drink?"

I watched her as she studied the gathering on the deck. Her face didn't give away any of her thoughts.

As I studied her, I hoped my face was as closed as hers. Detective Murdoch was tall, with an athletic build, as attractive as she was, I wondered why she had become a cop. With her looks she could have easily been a model or a movie star. What led her into law enforcement? And even more importantly, why was I so attracted to this annoying woman, especially since I'm sure she suspects me of murder?

My thoughts were interrupted by the detective's question. "What have you got that's non-alcoholic?"

"Ginger Ale, Root Beer…"

"Root Beer sounds good."

"Would you like a glass?"

"Hmmm. Is it can or bottle?"

"Bottle."

"Then I don't need a glass."

Moments later we joined the others on the deck, and I began the introductions. "Harriet Walsh, this is Detective Murdoch." I looked at the detective. "Detective Murdoch, is Detective your first name?"

Murdoch held my gaze. "No, my first name is Angela."

I grinned. "An appropriate name for a law enforcement officer."

"Oh. Why is that?"

I let the name roll off my tongue as if I were caressing it. "Angela, means messenger of God."

Brian Scott cleared his throat, and the moment was gone.

"Harriet owns My Place, the tea and coffee café down the road." Glancing at Harriet I added, "She makes the most delicious Madeleines."

"I'm not sure what a Madeleine is, but you make great donuts and excellent coffee. It's nice to officially meet you Harriet. I've been in a time or two to grab a coffee to go."

Harriet stood up and shook the detective's hand. "Yes, I remember you. Large coffee, black, to go, and about once a week you get a cake donut."

Det. Murdoch looked surprised. "Do you remember all of your customer's orders?"

Harriet laughed. "If they come in regular and order the same thing, then yes."

"And this" I indicated the Belgian Malinois sitting next to Harriet "is Cleo. She's a delightful creature and I'm eager to see if she and his feline majesty will get along."

Murdoch offered her hand to Cleo, who promptly responded with her paw. "Nice to meet you Cleo."

Laurel indicated Amber and Brian. "I'm sure you already know Brian and Amber."

With a confused expression, Det. Murdoch looked at me and said, "No, I'm afraid I've never had the pleasure."

Damn! I was hoping to get her to admit to knowing these two. "I happened to see both of them entering your office just the other day and considering how small it is, I figured you might have met them." I paused, giving anyone who wanted to say something the opportunity to do so. "However, since you haven't met, let me introduce, Brian Scott and Amber Hoffner. They're both computer geeks thinking of moving to our lovely town, evidently they're tired of the big city life."

Det. Murdoch nodded at the two. "Amber, Brian, nice to meet you." Brian stood up and shook her hand. "If you don't mind my asking, what were you in the station for? I hope it wasn't anything serious."

Amber stood up next to Brian and said, "No, we just wanted to check out the crime rates in a particular neighborhood where we're looking at houses. Cadet Donner was quite helpful."

"Glad to hear she was able to help you." A slight frown creased the detective's brow. "And it's good that you're being careful and checking out the neighborhoods. You can't be too careful these days, even in a small town."

Not liking the direction Murdoch was taking the conversation, I indicated all the vacant seats on the deck. "Let's all sit down and get acquainted for a few minutes and then I'll start the grill and get the steaks underway." The last thing I wanted to think about this evening were the murders of Natalie Kramer and the unidentified man.

Harriet asked Murdoch. "How come there's no Coventry Beach Police Department?"

Murdoch smiled. "That's a pretty common question. The short answer is the city couldn't afford to maintain its own police department, so they contract with the county and the Sheriff's Department supplies all law enforcement."

I chimed in. "How big an area do you cover, detective?"

"All of Coventry Beach and all of the county area between here and Darwin Springs, the county seat."

The evening moved along pleasantly with all the newcomers quizzing Murdoch about the area and then talking about how the places they had previously lived compared to Coventry Beach. The two recent murders weren't brought up by anyone.

The group was just finishing up the lovely Madeleines and tea that Harriet brought for dessert when Det. Murdoch's phone went off. She looked at the screen and sighed. "Excuse me. I have to take this." Moments later, the group watched Det. Murdoch pull the phone away from her face and look at the screen. She exhibited no reaction to what was on the screen and within seconds she put the phone back to her ear. Though no one at the table spoke the sound of the surf and the rustling of the plants in the light ocean breeze drowned out the detective's words.

Returning to the table, Murdoch stood behind her chair. Her phone was still in her hand. She looked over the complement at the table, from Harriet to the love birds and then her eyes stopped on me.

I found it interesting that when she straightened her shoulders, she moved her eyes to Brian as she stated, "There's been another murder." She held up a hand to forestall the many questions she could see coming. "Not in Coventry Beach. A body was found down in South Cove Beach, which is close enough that the locals think it could be connected to the murders here." She looked around the table at the reactions.

Harriet reached down and placed a hand on Cleo, as if to assure herself that her friend was there. Brian and Amber looked at each other. Amber squeezed his hand and said, "Maybe we should just stay in the big city, if there are this many murders in such a small-town, we're no safer here than in D.C."

I closed my eyes and shook my head in disbelief. I swallowed hard, opened my eyes, and asked, "Why do they think this murder might be connected?"

Det. Murdoch glanced down at the phone in her hand and then looked at me. "The victim fits the description of one of the women you described when you reported the stabbing on the beach." She paused. "I'm going to show you a picture of the latest victim. I need you to tell me if you recognize her."

I nodded my head and sat up straighter in my chair. Det. Murdoch fiddled with her phone for a moment and then turned it so I could see the screen.

I clapped a hand over my mouth and closed my eyes. Harriet who was sitting next to me, also saw the photo and shot to her feet so quickly her chair skidded back several feet before toppling over. Cleo immediately rose to stand next to her mistress.

Harriet turned to face the ocean. Her hand at her throat she asked, "Was that woman beheaded?"

Murdoch turned the phone back to herself and saw the picture the two women had seen. It was of the victim still buried up to her neck with a small crab perched on her head at her hairline. "My sincere apologies, ladies. That wasn't the picture I intended for you to see."

Alternating between fingering her necklace and stroking her throat, Harriet turned to face the detective. "It certainly looked like she was."

Murdoch pursed her lips as a V-shape formed between her brows. She drew in a deep breath. "No, she wasn't beheaded. I can't tell you the cause of death because we won't be certain until after the autopsy." She hesitated. "Since I'm sure the people that found her have already talked to the press, I can tell you she was found buried up to her neck down in South Cove Beach."

Realizing the implications of how the woman was found I pulled both of my lips into my mouth and swallowed several times. Murdoch walked around the table and stood behind my chair. "Please, take a look at this picture and tell me if you recognize this woman."

Murdoch was so close I could feel her breath on my neck and smell the fact that she must have showered just before coming to the party. Fresh soap and the smell of salt air mingled on her skin. I took a deep breath of her, which made concentrating on the picture difficult.

The young woman was lying on a steel table covered with a white sheet up to her shoulders. The picture showed her face and shoulders. While it wasn't as disturbing as the image of the disembodied head of the previous picture, it was obvious she was dead.

I forced myself to study the woman's face. Finally, I said, "I can't be sure. It might be the woman who witnessed the stabbing." I paused and gently pushed the phone away. "Do you have any pictures of her when she was alive?"

"No, I'm sorry. We haven't identified her yet."

Harriet turned to Murdoch. "May I see the photo?"

Murdoch held her gaze for a moment. Making sure it was the correct picture this time, she turned the screen toward Harriet.

Harriet tilted her head this way and then that way and finally said, "I believe she's been a regular in the shop for the past few weeks." She shrugged. "Like Laurel, I'd be able to tell better if it were a picture of her alive."

Murdoch put the phone away. "Harriet, close your eyes and try to picture her at your counter." She paused and waited a couple of heartbeats. "What is she ordering?"

Harriet did as Murdoch requested and soon, she said, "Yes, I think I can help you detective. We'll have to go to the café. If it's who I think it is, she was in yesterday afternoon. She always pays with a card and always orders a Cuban coffee and a raspberry danish." She looked around at the rest of us. "Sorry to break up the party."

"No apologies necessary. If you can help find out who killed that young woman you should." I looked at Brian and Amber. "Maybe you're right. You're no safer here than in the big city."

At the front door Murdoch turned to me. "Thank you for the lovely evening, Ms. Carpenito. I'm sorry to be the cause of it's premature ending."

CHAPTER 26

Harriet unlocked the front door of My Place. She and Murdoch walked through the dark dining area.

"If I remember correctly, she was in yesterday, right after my lunch rush, and ordered a Cuban coffee and a Danish." Harriet paused. "If it's who I'm thinking of that's what she orders every time."

As Harriet looked through the credit card receipts on her computer, Murdoch stood in the doorway. Lying on the floor next to the desk, Cleo watched Murdoch closely.

Murdoch indicated the dog and asked, "How well trained is she?"

Smiling Harriet looked down at Cleo. "She's very well trained and with all that's going on around here I may start bringing her to work with me." She returned to her computer search and moments later, said, "Ariel Fenton." She printed out the little information the credit card processor provided and handed it to Det. Murdoch.

"Thanks." Murdoch started for the exit but then paused. "You all right to get home?"

Cleo moved with Harriet as she stood up from her desk. "Yes, I'll be fine."

Harriet let Cleo into the front seat, climbed into the cab of the truck, locked the door behind her, and started the engine. She waved at Det. Murdoch who was sitting in her car in the parking lot. As Harriet pulled out of the parking lot, she glanced in her rearview mirror and saw Murdoch was driving down the road toward her office.

CHAPTER 27

At the back door to the sub-station, Murdoch punched in the appropriate code to unlock the door. Stepping inside the fluorescent lit breakroom she was happy to see it was empty. At the coffee station and she started to pour a cup of coffee but changed her mind. After the delightful tea Harriet had provided at the party, the idea of what passed for coffee here, wasn't appealing.

She dumped out the small amount of coffee she'd already poured, rinsed the cup, and put it back on the shelf.

In her office, she found FBI Special Agent Brian Scott waiting for her. Like Harriet, Murdoch didn't care much for the man. Like most federal agents he had a low opinion of local law enforcement and in his case it showed. "What are you doing here, Scott?"

"Protecting a multi-year investigation." He stood up and asked, "Did you get an identity for the woman?"

"We'll know in a few minutes." She said as she logged in to her computer. A search of the national and state criminal databases gave her nothing. Florida DMV was her next resource.

"Bingo! Ariel Fenton."

Agent Scott moved around the desk so he too could see the monitor. "She looked a lot better when she was alive."

"You think so?" Her sarcasm was totally lost on FBI Special Agent Scott.

Murdoch typed the victim's name and basic information into an email for Det. Carlton of the South Cove Beach Police Department, who was working the case.

"What are you doing?" Brian asked.

Standing up, Murdoch moved into Scott's personal space. He moved back a step. "I'm doing my job – what are you doing?"

Scott's jaw muscles twitching, he said in a tight voice. "I'm protecting a three-year investigation from getting mucked up by amateurs." He moved away from Murdoch and began pacing in front of her desk, like a caged tiger. Murdoch watched him as he clenched and unclenched his hands.

I suppose I should be used to being insulted by the men in my profession, but it still hurts.

Clamping her jaw shut so she wouldn't say something she would regret, Murdoch thought about the various insults she'd received over her years in law enforcement. Being called an amateur was a new one. Before she could form a civil response, FBI Special Agent Brian Scott, continued, "Before you go broadcasting the identity of this latest victim we need to determine if she's connected to our case."

"This was personal. Human traffickers aren't going to bury someone up to their necks in the sand and wait for the tide to come in and drown them." She fought to keep her voice from reaching the higher ranges, that men tend to describe as hysteria. "She was shot in the knee to keep her from escaping, then planted like a god damn tree. This woman watched the tide gradually creep up on her, with no way to escape." She took a deep breath. "This was very personal to whoever killed her, and they didn't care if the body was found. As a matter of fact, they wanted the body to be found. That stretch of beach doesn't get a lot of traffic but there are always people jogging or bike riding that make it that far south." She paused and sighed. "Not to mention the kids that wander down there from the park."

"Fine. Just don't give her identity to the press, yet."

"That will be up to Det. Carlton down in South Cove. He's the one handling the case." She sat back down at her keyboard to finish typing the email to Det. Carlton. Agent Scott stood glaring at her over her desk. His pacing had stopped but he continued to clench and unclench his hands.

Maintaining a poker face Murdoch worded the request to withhold the victim's identity from the public in such a way that she knew it would piss off Carlton. He still felt women should be kept barefoot and pregnant. She hit send and logged off before Agent Scott could come around the desk to see exactly what she had written.

Moments later a printout of Ariel Fenton's DMV photo came off the printer. Murdoch picked up the printout, and without a word pushed past FBI Special Agent Scott.

"Where are you going?"

"To do my job." She said without a backward glance.

CHAPTER 28

Murdoch parked her car in Laurel Carpenito's driveway, tripping the security lights for the entire front of the house.

With a wry smile, she thought, so much for an inconspicuous arrival.

She got out of the car and walked to the front door. Before she could ring the doorbell, the door opened.

"Please, come in detective."

Laurel was barefoot, dressed in light cotton pants and a loose-fitting oversized rust colored t-shirt that brought out the green in her eyes.

She closed the door, leaned against it, and turned to face Murdoch. "So, have you come to arrest me?"

Shaking her head, Murdoch asked, "Why do you think I might be here to arrest you?"

With a nervous laugh Laurel ran her hands through her short hair. It was a mannerism of hers Murdoch had noticed before and she liked the shy smile that came with it.

"Seems I used up all my good luck on winning the lottery. Ever since then it's been nothing but bad luck. But you didn't come here to listen to me whine about my misfortunes."

The detective watched her walk to the kitchen and noticed that she moved with the confidence of a woman who knows herself.

Reaching the stove just as the tea kettle began to whistle, Laurel asked, "Would you like some tea? It's the stuff Harriet brought for the party." She poured the hot water over the brew basket in the teapot. "It'll take a few minutes to steep."

Looking into Laurel's eyes, she said, "Some things are worth waiting for." Murdoch cleared her throat, looked away, and took a seat on one of the low backed stools at the breakfast bar. "I'm partial to coffee but since it's Harriet's tea, yes, I'd love a cup."

Laurel was glad her t-shirt was loose fitting, it kept Murdoch from seeing her nipples harden. Why does she have this effect on me? How can I be attracted to a woman who considers me a murder suspect?

A tense silence filled the room

Laurel uncovered the plate with the few remaining Madeleines, pushed the plate toward Murdoch, and handed her a teacup. "If you're not here to arrest me, to what do I owe the pleasure of your company?

"These are so much better than a cake donut." Murdoch took one of the delightful cakes and nibbled at it. "About that, why do you think I might be here to arrest you?"

Laurel turned away to brush non-existent crumbs off the kitchen counter. It kept Murdoch from seeing the warm flush she could feel moving up her body as she thought about Murdoch nibbling on her instead of a Madeleine. She rolled her head on her neck to relieve some of the building tension. "Suspicion of murder?"

"No, I don't think you killed Natalie Kramer."

Laurel turned to face Murdoch. "Oh, what about the unknown man on the beach?"

The two women held each other's gaze across the breakfast bar.

Meow. Tut voiced his displeasure at being left out of the conversation and jumped up on the bar. The spell was broken, and Laurel grabbed the cat, and placed him on the floor. She opened the treat jar and scattered a handful of treats on the kitchen floor.

When she straightened up, she poured tea into the teacups she had set out and asked, "For not telling you my real name?"

Murdoch washed down the moist lemon-flavored cake with a swallow of tea. "Yes, I suppose I could take you in for lying to a police officer, especially since you signed that formal statement with a false name."

Laurel smiled over her teacup. "Did I?"

Murdoch laughed. "You signed it with your legal name, didn't you?"

Setting the teacup down, Laurel held the detective's gaze. "My signature is such a scribble and my handwriting so awful I could have signed it with your name, and no one would know it." She paused. "However, I did verbally claim that my name is Laurel Carpenito."

Laurel freshened both cups of tea as she continued, "How about this, so that you're not compromised by helping me perpetuate my false identity, you call me by my initials."

"LC? Clever. The initials are correct for either name."

She smiled. "I did that intentionally, so I didn't have to worry about anything that was monogrammed. Truthfully, I can't take credit for it. It was my lawyer's idea."

"I actually came by on another matter." Murdoch pulled the printout of the DMV photo of Ariel Fenton from a folder and placed it on the bar. "Do you recognize her?"

Laurel picked up the photo and studied it. "Yes." She put the picture down. "She was the woman who witnessed the stabbing. Who is she?"

"Her name is Ariel Fenton. Ring any bells?"

"No. Can you tell me how she died?" She shuddered. "That first picture was...I don't even know how to describe the horror..."

Thinking about the pictures of Ariel Fenton's corpse put a damper on thoughts of Murdoch nibbling on her.

Even though it went against everything Murdoch knew as a cop, she told Laurel. "She was shot in the knee, we figure it was done to keep her from escaping while the hole was dug, and then she was buried with only her head above the sand. She watched as the tide rose to drown her." The detective kept her voice unemotional and watched Laurel for a reaction. "Until the autopsy is complete we won't know the actual cause of death."

Laurel's eyes grew wide, and she took several deep breaths. She ran her hands up and down her arms, as if she were trying to warm herself. "What a horrible way to die? Who would do such a horrific thing to another human being?" She shuddered. "And you think whoever did this, stayed to watch this woman drown?"

Looking at the picture of the attractive young woman known as Ariel Fenton, Murdoch said, "In this job I see the worst of humanity, but I have to admit, this is one of the worst things I've seen."

Laurel's voice was shaking as she asked, "What must this woman have done to inspire such hatred?"

Murdoch shrugged. "I don't know the reasoning behind it, assuming there was any reason involved. I only know it's my job to find out who, the why is only important if it helps me catch the who."

Another awkward silence inserted itself between the two women and then they both began to speak at once.

"It's your house, so you should speak first."

"I'm not sure about the logic behind that statement. Usually, the guest is given priority. However, despite what you said earlier, I know I'm a suspect in Natalie Kramer's murder and I suppose I can understand that, but I hope I'm not even a person of interest in this…insanity."

A soft smile moved Murdoch's lips upward. "No, I'm certain that no one suspects you in the Ariel Fenton case. Personally, I don't think you killed Natalie Kramer or the unidentified man on the beach either."

Murdoch swallowed the last of her tea and holding Laurel's gaze, continued. "But I'm not the only one investigating these cases."

CHAPTER 29

Detective Frank Carlton of the South Cove Beach Police Department opened the email from Detective Murdoch.

Wonder what the holier-than-thou great Detective Murdoch has to say.

He read and re-read the email identifying the Jane Doe from the beach as Ariel Fenton.

The line he kept re-reading was the one that said, "DO NOT release victim's identity to the press." Though his computer skills were limited, even he knew that all caps were the equivalent of yelling at a person.

"Yeah, that'll happen. I'll be damned if that bitch is going to tell me how to run my investigation" he muttered under his breath.

An officer walking by his office stopped. "You say something, detective."

He looked up from the computer screen. "Yeah, have we notified next of kin on this Ariel Fenton case?"

"Which case is that detective?"

One side of his mouth went up in a crooked smile. "Never mind kid. I think we need to ask for the public's help on this one." He stood up and studying the photo of Ariel Fenton said, "I think it's time for a conversation with Miss Conklin."

The officer was still standing in his doorway wearing a confused expression. "Conklin? Isn't that the reporter who's always…"

"Don't you have something to file?" snapped Carlton.

CHAPTER 30

Later that night, Susie Conklin, the news anchor for the local television station was in her element.

"Good evening and thank you for joining us tonight. The South Cove Beach Police Department is asking for the public's help."

Ariel Fenton's DMV photo filled half of the screen next to the anchorwoman.

"This is a picture of Ariel Fenton. The police are looking for relatives or friends of this latest crime victim. If you know anything about this woman please, contact Det. Frank Carlton of the South Cove Beach Police Department. As of this report, the police have been unable to find any friends or relatives. The police department's hotline number is scrolling across the bottom of your screen. If you know anything about this woman, please, call the hotline and ask for Det. Frank Carlton."

She paused, Ariel Fenton's picture disappeared, and Susie once again filled the screen.

"In other news…"

CHAPTER 31

Susie Conklin's report on Ariel Fenton had barely ended when Det. Angela Murdoch's phone rang.

FBI Special Agent Brian Scott wasted no time before calling her to give her a ration of his superiority and lambast her for incompetence for allowing Ariel Fenton's identity to be broadcast on television.

She sent him to voice mail.

I'll listen to it later. I doubt it's anything I want to hear anyway.

A few minutes later her phone notified her that she had a voicemail. After listening to the X-rated message FBI Special Agent Brian Scott left for her, she saved the message. Happy that she hadn't answered his call, Murdoch took several deep breaths to calm down from his tirade.

I wonder how Amber tolerates working with such an asshole.

CHAPTER 32

Social media picked up the Ariel Fenton report and ran with it. In less than twenty-four hours the South Cove Beach Police Department was flooded with phone calls, most of which were from attention seekers. The most promising ones were quickly checked out, which is why Det. Frank Carlton was standing at the front door of a Joanna Grange.

"Miss Grange?"

The older woman standing in the doorway was dressed in a pair of jeans, a polo shirt, tennis shoes, and an excessive amount of bangle bracelets. "Yes, I'm Mrs. Grange." She emphasized the 'Mrs.'. "And you are?"

He pointed to the gold shield hanging from his shirt pocket. "Det. Frank Carlton with South Cove Beach Police Department. You called us about Ariel Fenton."

Mrs. Grange looked over his shoulder and he turned to follow her gaze. The only thing she could be looking at was the house across the street. She brought her attention back to him and quickly ushered him into her house.

Once the door was closed, she relaxed. Her agitation over the house across the street and the obvious drop in her anxiety level once they were inside didn't escape his notice.

It took several seconds for his eyes to adjust to the low light level in the house. He thought that the light level in the house would be well-suited for a vampire. The windows were all covered with heavy drapes keeping out the bright Florida sunlight.

I don't understand why all the old people I run into want to keep their house so damn dark. If you don't like the sun, move somewhere that doesn't have so much sun. Crazy old lady.

"Please, have a seat, Det. Carlton." She led him into the living room where she daintily put herself in an old-fashioned wing-back chair and motioned for him to occupy the chair opposite hers. "How may I help the South Cove Beach Police Department today?"

At six feet two inches and 230 pounds, he hesitated to sit on the chair she indicated. The small wood chair with the rattan seat looked delicate and fragile. However, he wasn't about to insult the woman. She looked like the type that would file a complaint in a heartbeat. He gently lowered himself into the chair and tried to ignore the creaking complaints it made as he settled onto the seat.

"As I said, you contacted us in reference to Ariel Fenton." She looked confused. "The woman whose picture was on the news," he prompted.

"Oh yes, that poor woman." She remained silent for several moments before continuing, "She was a pretty little thing. No bigger than a minute." She snorted. "Certainly, nothing like that Amazonian wife of his."

Carlton leaned forward in the chair, realizing that this might be a legitimate lead. Ariel Fenton had indeed been a very petite young woman. "Who is this man you're referring to?"

She sniffed as if she had caught a whiff of something unpleasant. "Mr. Bates, across the street." She sat up straighter in her chair. "He and his wife moved here just a few months ago. Not long after they arrived, I began to notice that whenever his wife was out this young lady would visit Mr. Bates." That look of having smelled something rotten crossed her face again. "But you know I haven't seen him in, oh, at least several days. Of course, since he wasn't around you would think that his girlfriend wouldn't come around either." She sighed. "But then just the other day, I saw his wife and his girlfriend going into the house together."

"The wife and the husband's girlfriend?"

"Yes, that's what I said. Don't you think that's a bit strange, detective?" Her voice was very light and her enunciation precise. It reminded him of his English teacher in high school.

Using the non-writing end of his pen he scratched his head. "Yes, ma'am." Carlton stood up and moved to the nearest window. He started to pull the drapes back at the edge to get another look at the house across the street.

"No!" Mrs. Grange screamed. "Don't do that, please. She might see you."

He immediately let the drape fall back into place and returned to his chair. It was obvious the Mrs. Grange was terrified of her neighbor.

"You see, she's really a well I'm not sure what to say about her, really." Mrs. Grange played with the bangles around her wrist, fingering them noisily. "She's threatened me, you know."

"I'm sorry to hear that ma'am. Why did she threaten you?"

Mrs. Grange shifted in her chair, straightened her posture again and said, "I was getting my mail and her husband was at their mailbox getting their mail. I was simply being neighborly. It's good to know who your neighbors are, so I was asking about him. You know what kind of work he did or was he retired."

"What kind of work was he into?"

Mrs. Grange sniffed and harrumphed. "I never found out because his wife came storming out of the house, screaming that if she ever caught me flirting with her husband again, she'd kill me." She smiled at Carlton and continued, "As if I would have any interest in a short balding man with a belly." Her eyes ran over

Carlton's body the way a hungry person eyes a meal. "Now you on the other hand…"

Frank Carlton knew what he looked like. High cheek bones, a strong jaw, and puppy dog eyes went a long way toward making sure he had no trouble getting dates. Despite his years at a desk, he managed to keep himself in good shape and thanks to the genes his parents gave him he still had a full head of luxurious black hair.

Ignoring the inuendo he asked, "Can you give me her full name and a description?"

"I believe Mr. Bates called her Edith. She's close to six feet tall, for a woman she has broad shoulders, her hair is cut short. Almost like a helmet, but it does have a slight wave to it." She put a finger to the side of her face and looked up at the ceiling. Bringing the finger down to point at Carlton she said, "Quite often there's a curl that comes down the middle of her forehead."

Every cop in the state had a copy of the sketches from the Coventry Beach murder witness. Carlton pulled his out, glanced at it and showed it to Mrs. Grange.

She took the paper from him and turned on the table lamp closest to her. She studied it for so long, he was beginning to wonder if she was trying to memorize it. "It does look a great deal like her."

Carlton suppressed a smile that threatened to engulf his entire face. The idea of solving Murdoch's case for her was almost too good to be true. He pulled out another picture. Clearing his throat, he tried to contain his excitement. "Do you recognize this man?"

Mrs. Grange returned the first picture as she accepted the second one. "That's a very good likeness of Mr. Bates." She looked up from the picture and held his gaze. Her voice was quiet, and her eyes expressed sadness. "He's dead, isn't he?"

"Yes, ma'am. I'm afraid he is." He spoke in an authoritative voice. "Mrs. Grange, I'm going to need you to stay in your house, until I tell you it's safe to come out."

The frail older woman seemed to sink into the chair. "Oh dear. What do you mean? Do you think she'll come after me for talking to you?"

He smiled and tried to calm her fears. "No, ma'am. It's just a precaution. I'm going to go over and talk to Mrs. Bates about her husband."

With pleading eyes Mrs. Grange looked up at him. "Please, go talk to some of the other neighbors first. I don't want her to think I'm the only one that you could have gotten your information from."

* * * *

Why is there an unmarked cop car at that old biddy's house? Of course, last night's news. Busybody must have recognized that scrawny little bitch and called the cops. Damn it! I don't have time to deal with cops and I'm not ready to leave town yet. I've got to deal with another nosey parker before I move on.

Edith Bates looked through the slats of the window blinds. Still no sign of the cop. She turned and gave the house a quick once over.

Nothing here I need to take with me. I'm out of here.

* * * *

As Det. Carlton stepped out of Mrs. Grange's house, he stopped on the porch long enough to call for backup. Dispatch told him a patrol car was five minutes away.

I followed protocol. I called for backup but seriously, it's one woman. I'm not waiting for uniforms to show up.

132

Hooking the police radio on his belt, he started toward the Bates' house. Carlton reached the sidewalk in front of Mrs. Grange's house when he saw the garage door of the Bates' house going up.

Well, at least I won't have to worry about no one answering the door.

Most people back out of their garage, so he headed for the side of the driveway where he expected the driver of the car to be. By the time he realized that the car was coming out nose first it was too late to move to the other side of the driveway.

He called out in his most authoritative voice, "Mrs. Bates, I'm Det. Frank Carl..."

The car suddenly sped up and headed straight for him. He dove for the grass and almost made it unscathed.

As he watched the car speed away, he was able to tell the license plate was from Rhode Island. The distinctive wave of that state's license plate and the first two letters, BB were all he was able see before the car was too far away.

Lying on the grass, he reached for the police radio on his belt. It wasn't there. Looking around he spotted it in the grass, several feet away. He started to get up but quickly found his right leg wouldn't tolerate his weight and he collapsed in pain.

Breathing heavily from the pain and exertion, he used his arms to pull himself across the yard to the communication device.

When he reached it, he pressed the button but didn't hear the familiar sound of connection.

"Shit!" Getting bounced around on the ground must have damaged it.

He flopped onto his back and started digging in his pocket for his cell phone as a patrol car pulled up to the curb.

CHAPTER 33

That evening the news didn't report how Det. Frank Carlton had captured a woman suspected of two murders, instead Susie Conklin, once again appealed to the public. This time she shared the screen with an image of Edith Bates.

"This woman, Edith Bates, is considered dangerous. The South Cove Beach Police Department asks that you not attempt to apprehend but rather that you notify them immediately if you see this woman." As she spoke, her image was replaced with the video shot earlier of Det. Carlton being loaded into an ambulance. "South Cove Beach Police Detective Frank Carlton, was the victim of a hit and run earlier today as he attempted to speak with Edith Bates about the death of her husband, Warren Bates."

CHAPTER 34

Det. Angela Murdoch was tired and in need of a cup of coffee, so she stopped at My Place for an evening cup of decaf to take home. Like a woman on a mission, she headed straight for the counter without a glance around the place. She already knew that Laurel was inside. Her electric blue Prius was in the parking lot.

If I'm lucky she'll be too involved in her own thoughts to even notice I'm in the place. I'll get my coffee and head home. All I really want right now is to get some sleep. And maybe in the morning I can figure out how I managed to give the credit for solving two murders to Frank Carlton?

As she walked to the counter, she continued to mentally rearrange the steps she'd taken, removing some and altering the way she had handled others. Every time the only way the outcome was different was if she had listened to FBI Special Agent Brian Scott and kept the latest victim's identity to herself.

Of course, that would have meant that we most likely still wouldn't know who our dead man was or have any idea of who killed him. Not acceptable. Better that misogynist Neanderthal get the credit than to have Edith Bates get away with two murders. Although thanks to his arrogance that murdering bitch is still on the loose.

Harriet strolled out of the kitchen and greeted Murdoch with a smile. "Good evening, detective."

"If you say so," she growled in reply. Harriet's eyebrows rose in surprise at the brusque response.

Murdoch sighed and tried to smile, resulting in the slightest upturn of her lips at the corners. "I'm sorry. I'm afraid I'm not particularly good company right now."

Harriet smiled. "You just solved a murder, actually two. I should think you'd be in a fine mood. What's the trouble?"

"First, we have no proof that Edith Bates is guilty of anything."

Laurel had moved to the counter to stand next to Murdoch. "Seriously? At the very least she's guilty of trying to run down Det. Carlton."

Murdoch looked at her. "Carlton can't ID the driver," and then turned back to Harriet. "The sun was reflecting off the windshield."

"Wow!" Harriet shook her head. "You know the woman killed her husband and probably the girlfriend too."

"Knowing it and proving it are two very different things. We did get a search warrant for the Bates house and hopefully the forensics team will find something there." She knew her voice was giving away her lack of faith in the forensics crew, but she was so tired she really didn't care.

"Regardless, I" she put a strong emphasis on the last word "am not the one that solved either of those murders." Her voice showed all the bitterness she felt. "Det. Frank Carlton solved them."

Harriet tilted her head to one side. "Without your cooperation..."

"...and my descriptions of the two women, he wouldn't have been able to solve anything," Laurel added.

Murdoch's lips curled up higher into a full smile as she turned to Laurel.

"Face it, Det. Murdoch, without your willingness to share information with another agency we still wouldn't know who the stabbing victim was or who, most likely, murdered him, and I have no doubt that you'll find a way to prove it." Smiling, back at Murdoch, Laurel continued, "Carlton may have figured out who the killer was, but he also let her get away and got himself injured in the process."

"Let's hope the Sheriff sees it that way."

Harriet glanced at the wall clock behind her. "It's closing time." She moved to the front door locked it, turned off the open sign, and closed all the blinds, as she spoke, "I made some chicken pot pies and I hate to eat alone. If you two will set a table, I'll bring them from the kitchen."

While Murdoch was still tired, she realized she was also hungry, besides, she knew there was no sense in arguing with Harriet.

The three women sat in the café enjoying each other's company and Harriet's delicious chicken pot pies, accompanied by a special tea blend that was Harriet's own creation.

Laurel said, "You know Harriet, while I've always liked an occasional cup of tea, you could almost, almost get me to give up coffee."

Murdoch laughed. "Yeah, don't tell any of my fellow officers but I agree with LC."

No one made any mention of Natalie Kramer's murder. Murdoch didn't want to bring it up because at the present time Laurel was still a person of interest in the case. Laurel didn't want to bring it up because she knew she was a suspect and Harriet just didn't want to talk about anything so unpleasant.

Murdoch made certain that both women were safely on the way to their respective homes before pulling out of the café's parking lot. As she drove to her apartment, thoughts of Laurel Carpenito's soft laughter and twinkling eyes flitted through her mind.

CHAPTER 35

Harriet reached over and petted Cleo, who wore her own special seat belt in the front passenger seat. As they drove home, she wondered why Det. Murdoch and Laurel didn't see the attraction that existed between them. Shaking her head at the blindness of some people, she spoke to Cleo. "Maybe they do see it and they're fighting it. What do you think, girl?"

Cleo looked at her and gave one soft, short bark.

"Yes, I agree. We'll have to see if we can't help them find each other."

CHAPTER 36

Once home I started the water in the tea kettle heating. Figuring I had enough time before the water boiled, I headed upstairs where I changed into a pair of cargo shorts and a t-shirt. Tut followed me up the stairs and lay on the bed watching as I dressed in more comfortable clothes.

My hand hovered over the 9mm on the nightstand. I contemplated leaving it there but thought better of it and placed it in the large front pocket of the shorts. Feeling its weight pulling on the shorts, I added a belt and then headed down to the kitchen.

I arrived just as the tea kettle began to whistle. Tut jumped up on the breakfast bar and watched as I poured the boiling water over the tea leaves in the brew basket. I put the special cozy Harriet had given me around the cup and set the timer on my phone.

I sure hope Harriet is right and this tea helps me sleep.

With teacup in hand, I moved to the deck. I closed the sliding glass door most of the way, turned on the turtle nesting season approved light, placed the teacup on the small table next to my chair, and sat down. I closed my eyes and took a deep breath of the salty night air. Moments later Tut wandered out and rubbed against my legs before jumping into my lap.

Absent-mindedly alternating between petting the small black feline and rubbing its ears I began to mentally review the events of the past several days.

Natalie Kramer wanders in claiming to be Carly Reddington. That night I find her body washed up on shore a few blocks from here. Right after that I have the dubious honor of witnessing a woman stab a man on the beach right here in front of my house. Then…

I silenced the timer for my tea just as a woman's voice called, "Hello the house." The voice came from the path to the beach. It had a bit of a southern accent but with so few words to work with I couldn't decide which of the southern states.

I slid Tut through the narrow opening of the sliding glass door, closed the door all the way, and stepped into the shadows at the other end of the screen enclosure.

"Who are you and what do you want?" I tried to keep my tone light and friendly, but I heard the harshness of apprehension in my words.

"My name is Terri Snokes. I'm head volunteer of the nighttime turtle patrol." She paused as if waiting for a reply.

Georgia or Alabama. Not that it matters. "Sorry if I seem less than friendly. There's been a lot going on around here lately."

I heard her draw a long deep breath. "Yeah, we've been traveling in pairs to patrol the beach ever since Natalie Kramer's body washed up on shore near a busted-up turtle nest."

She moved up to the screen door. "I try to get by and introduce myself to the new folks along the beach." My visitor smiled but instead of it coming off as friendly, it just looked macabre. The red light gave her teeth a look of being blood stained. It was an eerie sight, and I felt a chill run up my spine.

"That's nice. I'm sure the tourists appreciate you sharing your knowledge about the area." My phone rang. What I saw on the screen made me smile. Excellent timing.

"Good evening, Detective Murdoch. Yes, I made it home safely, as a matter of fact, I'm standing on my back deck talking with

Terri…" I stepped out of the shadows and smiled at Terri, "I'm sorry, I'm terrible with names what did you say your last name was?"

"Snokes. Terri Snokes." A flash of something like irritation moved across the woman's face. Or at least I thought I'd seen such an expression, but in the poor light conditions, I couldn't be sure. She smiled and called out, "Hello Murdoch."

When I disconnected the call, Terri said, "It's getting late and I should get back to patrolling, so I'll wish you a good night." She started to turn away, paused, and held out a business card. "If you see something on the beach you think I should know about feel free to call me."

I stepped up to the screen door, unlocked it, took the card, relocked the door, and said, "Thanks. Stay safe out there."

She smiled and nodded before turning and heading back down to the beach.

A moment later a question occurred to me and I spun around but she was already gone.

Deciding that I would drink my tea on the balcony I grabbed my cup, entered the house, and locked the sliding glass door. Tut jumped up on the bar and watched me as I turned off the lights, dumped my tea leaves, and checked that all the doors were locked.

Leaning on the bar, I scratched under the cat's chin. "So, my furry friend, if the turtle patrol is supposed to be working in pairs, where was Terri Snokes' patrol partner?"

I rubbed noses with him before bending down so that he could easily climb up and drape himself around my neck. "Alright, you handsome devil, let's go to bed."

CHAPTER 37

Tut and I were up before sunrise. Despite my misgivings about the previous night's visit from Terri Snokes, I had slept well. Knowing who was the true Alpha in the household I fed His Majesty before even starting the water for tea.

Although I was a still a coffee lover, there were mornings when what I really craved was a cup of Harriet's special blend, Lady Anna. This was one of those mornings, but I was out.

"Well crap, I guess I'll just have to go see Harriet." I looked at the time and knew that although My Place wasn't open for business yet, Harriet would be in the kitchen.

"Tut, old man. I'm getting dressed and leaving you to your own devices." Tut didn't even look up from his food dish.

Moments later I was dressed. I stuffed my wallet into one pocket, phone into another, grabbed my car keys, and was out the door.

It was first light, a good thirty minutes before sunrise so there was little traffic as I drove down the road to My Place.

I pulled into the parking lot behind the cafe, expecting to see Harriet's big truck, but the lot was empty. The hairs on the back of my neck stood up and I quickly drove around to the front of the building. No sign of Harriet.

I stayed in the car and called Harriet's cell. The call went straight to voicemail. I didn't leave a message, instead I immediately disconnected and called Murdoch.

"Good morning, Ms. Carpenito." Murdoch was a morning person, so she too was up and about, getting her day underway.

"Good morning, detective." Without pausing for any further pleasantries, I continued, "Have you heard from Harriet since we left her place last night?"

"No. Should I have?" The concern in her voice was plain to hear.

"I don't know. I'm sitting in the parking lot at My Place and she's not here. She's always here at least two hours before she opens."

"Maybe she had to go to the store and pick something up." Murdoch's voice told me she really didn't believe what she was saying.

"Nobody opens before Harriet. Something's wrong. I'm going to her house. Meet me there." I hadn't made it a request and I didn't wait for a reply before I ended the call.

Harriet only lived a few miles from My Place. I was there in less than five minutes. As I parked in front of the house Murdoch pulled up behind me.

My surprised expression brought a smile to Murdoch's face as she said, "I was headed to My Place for my morning coffee." She shrugged. "Harriet always lets me in early."

Murdoch rolled her shoulders as she surveyed the front of Harriet's house.

Harriet's big pick-up truck was in the driveway and yet the house gave me the feeling that it was empty. Everything about this felt wrong.

Murdoch said, "Wait here," as she moved toward the house.

Far more concerned about finding out what happened to my friend than in my own safety, I was right behind Murdoch. The detective sighed; she knew that saying something to me about waiting in my car would be a complete waste of breath. "Just make sure you stay behind me," she said in a resigned tone.

I gave a short nod of my head to signify agreement.

The concrete block home was typical old Florida. The crawl space under the house was about two feet high and open at the front of the house. There were five steps leading to the screened in porch. Murdoch knocked on the wood door frame.

"Harriet. Hello. Anybody home?" We were met with a silence that said no one was home. Murdoch tried the screen door. It was locked.

She hesitated and then turned to me and said, "Let's go around back."

I glanced to my right at the six-foot high vinyl fence that enclosed the backyard. "Sure, as long as you can figure a way over that fence." I moved back down the steps. "Harriet said she always keeps it locked because Cleo... Cleo hasn't announced us"

Murdoch led the way to the single gate and tried it. It was unlocked. We exchanged glances. Murdoch put her hand on her holstered sidearm and pushed the gate open.

Fifteen feet inside the yard Cleo was lying in the grass.

"No!" I raced past Murdoch and dropped to my knees next to the dog. Placing my hand on the dog I felt the rise and fall of her shallow breathing. Running my hands over the canine body I looked for any injury that might have caused this inertia.

On Cleo's rear haunch, close to her spine, I felt something hard. Carefully I pulled the fur back to reveal a piece of what looked like a dart.

"Is she dead?" Murdoch asked, standing behind me with her gun now drawn.

"No. It looks like somebody shot her with a tranquilizer dart." I petted the dog's head. "Poor baby, where's your momma?"

Murdoch called for backup. Looked around the side yard and said, "Stay with Cleo. Brighton's on his way."

Cleo began to come to, but I kept her lying down. "As soon as possible we need to get her to a vet."

Murdoch was already moving toward the back of the house, sweeping the view in front of her with her gun. I watched her go around the corner of the house.

Cleo whimpered. "Shhh. Sweet girl. We'll find your momma."

Murdoch still hadn't returned when I heard a car door close out front and through the open gate saw Deputy Brighton walk to the front door. I heard voices but couldn't make out the words. I watched as Brighton returned to his patrol car.

Moments later Murdoch walked back through the gate. "It looks like there's been a struggle." Her next words were rapid fire and emotionless, as if she were giving a report on the weather. "Some blood but not enough for anybody to be dead or dying from blood loss." She paused. "How's Cleo?"

Looking down at the dog, I said, "She's coming out of it but she's still groggy." Bringing my gaze up to Murdoch, "We need get her to a vet and get that dart removed before we let her walk around." I returned my attention to Cleo. "There's not enough of the dart above the skin to grab hold of with fingers but a vet will have the proper tools to remove it."

Murdoch knelt across from me, next to Cleo's head, she smiled as she looked into the dog's eyes. "That's why I've called a mobile vet I know. She'll be here in a few minutes." At the sound of a large van on the street Murdoch stood up. "That's probably her now."

A compact blonde woman came through the open gateway, surveyed the situation at a glance, and closed the gate. The black bag in her hand looked like the bags I remember seeing doctors carry on old television westerns.

She greeted Murdoch as she knelt next to Cleo. "Hey Murdoch, so this is the patient." The woman's southern accent was like warm honey dripping with butter.

"Yeah, her name's Cleo."

The new arrival opened her bag grabbed a stethoscope and listened to Cleo's breathing and heart. Then she expertly ran her hands over the dog's body and located the offending remnant of the dart. The entire time she was working on the dog, she was murmuring to her about what a good girl she was. Her voice was soothing and calming.

She reached into the black bag and pulled out what looked like a pair of needle-nose pliers. Addressing me, she said, "Be ready. She's probably going to jump." Turning her attention back to Cleo, she continued, "It'll be all right, sweetie. I wish I had gotten here sooner because then you wouldn't have felt this at all. You would have still been unconscious. I'm sorry but this will probably hurt a bit."

Holding down Cleo's hind quarters with one hand, she used the pliers to get a firm grip on the stub of the dart and yanked it out.

Cleo gave a small yelp and flinched.

The vet dropped the piece of dart into a plastic bag proffered by Murdoch, who sealed it, initialed, and dated the seal before putting the bag in a pocket.

I was still sitting on the grass with Cleo's head in my lap. The young blonde veterinarian looked at me and said, "Hi, I'm Peggy Lister. I operate a mobile vet service."

"I'm Laurel Carpenito. Will Cleo be okay?"

Peggy's hand, that was petting Cleo, paused for a second. She looked up from the dog to me. "More than likely. In a good part because she didn't continue to move around with that dart in her. It was too close to her spine for comfort." She returned her eyes to the dog and then back to me. "You're the woman who keeps finding dead bodies, aren't you?"

Before I could respond Cleo decided she had had enough of lying around. She lifted her head from my lap, looked around, and staggered to her feet.

Cleo's actions gave me a moment to think about how I was going to respond to Peggy's question.

The newspapers never printed my name. She's a friend of Murdoch's. Sounds like Murdoch's been blabbing about the case. I wonder how close those two are. Pillow talk?

As I got to my feet, I shot a glare at Murdoch. Putting a bland expression on my face I looked at Peggy and asked, "What makes you think so?"

Something in my tone, must have alerted her that I wasn't happy about being identified in such a manner. "I'm sorry honey. I didn't mean to upset you." Peggy looked from me to Murdoch and back. With a mischievous smile on her face she continued, "Murdoch described you so well" she shrugged "I just knew it had to be you that she's been working on these cases with."

Described me. Why in the world would she be describing me to this woman? Working on these cases with? Interesting phrasing.

Peggy winked at me and said, "Don't be too angry with her. I can assure you; she has no idea that she's put her foot in it." She glanced at her watch. "I have an appointment in ten minutes that's a good fifteen minutes from here. Time to go."

She held out a business card to me. "If you need anything, give me a call." She paused. "I wrote my personal cell number on the back." She turned to Murdoch. "Unless you need me for something else, I'm gone. I have a business to run, you know."

"Thanks, Peggy. I owe you one."

Peggy stopped at the gate and turned back. "You all come to the Red Pig, buy me a beer and a taco and we'll call it even."

"Done."

Without another word Peggy slipped out and closed the gate behind her.

I put the business card in a pocket. For a moment I stared at the closed gate, thinking about how to handle the situation of Murdoch describing me to another woman.

Too much to process right now. Need to focus on the problem at hand.

"Murdoch, what's going on? Where is Harriet?"

Murdoch rubbed the back of her neck. It was something I noticed her do whenever she was in a stressful situation. Her response wasn't reassuring. "I wish I knew."

Cleo barked, as if voicing the same question, I had just asked. I used the command I'd heard Harriet use to quiet the animal. Still unsteady on her four paws, Cleo turned and looked at me, walked over, and sat down next to me. For the time being, she had found her new Alpha.

Murdoch smiled. "Well, at least I don't have to worry about what to do with her while we search for Harriet."

With a sigh I glanced down at Cleo. "You do understand that you're going to be staying with a cat, who thinks he's a god."

Cleo's large dark eyes looked up at me as if to say, "It's okay. Tut and I will get along just fine."

Rubbing the top of Cleo's head, I said, "I'll need her harness, leash, food, and bed." I held up a hand to forestall any objections. "I doubt that any of those items are vital to your crime scene. If they are, let me know and I'll stop at the pet store on the way home but I'd rather Cleo had familiar items."

Murdoch sighed. "Give me a minute."

148

CHAPTER 38

Back home I left Cleo in the garage while I went into the house. Having no idea how the two animals would react to one another, I decided it would be best to introduce them slowly.

Tut was asleep in the living room recliner. I grabbed the cat carrier and put a groggy Tut into the soft sided cage and zipped it closed before he was aware of what was going on. He glared at me as if to say, you will pay for this later.

I sighed. "Yes, I know all about your feelings regarding the carrier, your majesty. However, I need to keep you safe in case Cleo thinks you're a chew toy." I placed the carrier on the floor, where as soon as Cleo came in, she would see it.

Tut retreated to the back of the carrier. Looking through the mesh sides I could see his back haunches bunched under him with his front paws, ready to spring at the first opportunity. I went back to the garage and brought Cleo in, on her harness and leash.

I closed the door to the garage. Cleo and I stood just inside the house. Cleo looked around, surveying the area quickly, sniffing the air. In a matter of seconds, her eyes landed on the cat carrier. I gave the leash some slack and Cleo stepped forward, her nose down to sniff the cage.

Since Cleo wasn't exhibiting any aggressive moves, I continued to give her more and more slack on the leash, until she was lying on the floor in front of the carrier.

Cleo was on her belly, front paws to either side of the carrier, and her nose pressed against its soft mesh material.

Tut crept forward. His nose was twitching and wrinkling, mouth open to pull the dog's smell across the appropriate scent organs. Cautiously, he reached a paw up to the front screen and lightly touched Cleo's nose.

Cleo turned her head from side-to-side, as if questioning why Tut was in the strange box. Cleo made a strange noise, not quite a whimper but definitely not a bark. Tut meowed back at her.

Under my breath I muttered, "Well I'll be damned. I do believe you two are going to get along." I grabbed the cat carrier from the floor, set it on the table, and unzipped the door. Cleo sat up and watched my every move. Tut stepped out of the carrier and sat down on the table.

More strange sounds came out of Cleo as she sat, as if at attention while Tut looked down at her from his spot on the table. Cleo stood and moved close to the table and placed her nose up against Tut's nose.

I wondered if they were talking with each other, as each was making barely audible sounds. Deciding that it was safe to leave the two alone, I returned to the garage to get the rest of Cleo's things.

CHAPTER 39

I was sitting at the bar searching the internet when the doorbell rang. "Come in, detective".

The door opened and Detective Murdoch stepped into the entranceway, quickly closing the door behind her. I appreciated her remembering that Tut was a flight risk. She removed her sunglasses and took in the scene before her.

Tut was sitting on the back of the recliner in the living room. Across the room Cleo stood at attention, waiting for input from her new Alpha, on how to treat Murdoch.

I looked up and said, "Skywalker." Cleo went to her bed and laid down.

The corners of Murdoch's mouth almost moved up into a smile. She moved her gaze from Cleo to me. "What would have happened if you said Dar…"

"I don't recommend you finish that sentence."

Murdoch's eyebrows rose questioningly.

"Because I'm not sure exactly what would happen, and I don't think either one of us wants to explain anything to your boss."

"Hmmmm. True." She glanced at Cleo, then brought her eyes back to me. "On another topic, do you always leave your front door unlocked?"

"Hardly and most definitely not, now that there's a crazy lady running around town." I sighed. "My camera system activated when you pulled into the driveway, so I unlocked the door."

Murdoch opened her mouth as if she were going to speak but then closed it without a word.

The silence between us lasted longer than I was comfortable with, finally I said, "What's going on with finding Harriet? Do you know who took her? Has any progress been made in finding her? You do know that she's been running from a stalker for the past two years, right?"

"Yes, Harriet told me about her former fiancé." Murdoch took a long, slow breath, and sat down on a bar stool. "The investigation is underway. Since it's an active investigation I can't tell you anything."

I watched her face. Her poker face wasn't working for her at the moment and it seemed like she wanted to tell me something. She took a deep breath. "The Sheriff has called in the FBI."

"The FBI? Is that normal?"

"Yes and no. He hates federal interference; however, we're already so shorthanded…"

"Well then, what I've done should be appreciated. I've hired search and rescue to help with the search." Before Murdoch could object, I continued, "This is a professional team who work with law enforcement on a regular basis. Don't tell me that your department can't afford to pay for them, I'm paying them. It's the least I can do to help find Harriet."

I held Murdoch's gaze, "Ever since Rachel – died…" speaking the word out loud for the first time, I felt a weight lift from me, as if I had shrugged off a coat, I hadn't realized I was wearing.

I lifted my shoulders, straightened my posture, and continued, "Harriet and I have become good friends. Harriet is the first person… Anyway, I want to do everything I can to help find her." I glanced at the wall clock and took a deep breath. "Your boss should be getting a call any minute now."

152

That damn poker face of hers was back and I couldn't tell what she was thinking.

"You think her ex-fiancé picked up her trail?"

"Yes. He's the reason she left New Orleans and has been running for almost two years. His name is Alan Henry." I paused. "You know all this, why do you seem hesitant to think it's him?"

Rather than answer my question, she changed the subject. "Exactly how do you think you're going to get something with Harriet's scent?"

Before I could reply, Murdoch's cell phone rang. She looked at the screen. "Excuse me."

I could only hear Murdoch's side of the conversation, but I knew what was happening. Murdoch ended the call and slid her phone back into her pocket.

"I suppose you're behind what I was just ordered to do."

I tilted my head a fraction and replied, "That depends on what it is you've been ordered to do." I watched the tightening of Murdoch's jaw and the way she narrowed her eyes.

Murdoch ignored the implied question. "Regardless of how well-intentioned, I don't think it's a good idea for civilians to, interfere with a police investigation. I'm sure you mean well, but…"

I stood up from my stool on the kitchen side of the bar. "I don't really give a rodent's rosy red rectum how you feel about my 'interference' in your precious investigation." I moved from the kitchen to the front door. "I care about getting Harriet back, safe and sound."

Murdoch rose and followed me. I started to open the door and paused. "On another subject, while I can't make you keep my real name to yourself, I'd appreciate it if you continued to do so."

We held each other's gaze for several seconds, neither of us spoke, then I opened the door.

153

From the way Murdoch peeled out of my driveway I must have really pissed her off. The rubber she left on the street would mean a new set of tires for her car if she kept driving like that.

CHAPTER 40

After the initial laying of rubber on the street in front of Laurel's house, Murdoch maintained a tight control of her driving.

How does that woman manage to push my buttons? It's like she's not even trying and yet every time I see her, I want to... No, I'm not falling for the poor little rich girl. Am I?

During the rest of the drive to Harriet's house, Murdoch tried to concentrate on her job; however, instead she spent the drive trying to convince herself that she wasn't attracted to Laurel Carpenito aka Larissa Carpenter.

Pulling up in front of Harriet's house Murdoch saw FBI Special Agent Brian Scott talking to a man with a bloodhound. The look on Scott's face showed his irritation and this brought a smile to Murdoch's face.

Anything that annoys that misogynist is fine by me. I wonder if he knows Laurel's real name. I can't imagine he doesn't. I do know he won't learn it from me.

The man dressed in khaki cargo pants with a bloodhound at his feet had his back to Murdoch. But the tension in his shoulders told her that FBI Special Agent Brian Scott was being his usual charming self.

Nice to know he annoys his own gender too.

She wasn't close enough to hear what bullshit Scott was spouting but it was obvious that he was giving the dog handler a hard time. If Scott's against it, I'm all for it.

Murdoch called out as she walked toward the pair. "Hi there. Great looking bloodhound."

Special Agent Scott snapped his mouth shut mid-word as the dog handler turned around. As his master moved the dog stood up and shifted position with him, as if he were a physical appendage of the man.

Murdoch liked animals better than most people, especially dogs.

"Hi, I'm Detective Murdoch."

He took her hand in a firm grip, shook it, and released it. She was instantly impressed by his ability to shake a woman's hand properly. His handshake was neither limp nor crushing.

"I'm Howard Barlow and this is Finder."

"Nice to meet you Mr. Barlow." She indicated the bloodhound. "May I pet Finder?"

"Yes, ma'am. He loves attention and please, call me Howard." He smiled. Like most people with pets, if you pay attention to their animals, and treat them right, they'll like you.

Murdoch bent down and scratched the top of Finder's head. "Finder you're a handsome fellow" she sighed "and I hope you live up to your name." She straightened up and held Howard's gaze.

"I understand you've been hired to try and find Harriet Walsh."

"Yes, ma'am. I need something that has the woman's scent on it."

Murdoch glanced past Howard to Special Agent Scott, who stood with his arms crossed, glaring at her.

Howard's voice brought her attention back to him. "I've been trying to explain to Special Agent Scott that Finder needs..."

"Just a moment, Howard." Murdoch moved past him toward Special Agent Scott. "How about if you explain the process to both of us?" Howard and Finder turned back to face Special Agent Scott and Murdoch. "Tell us about Finder's abilities. I know how this

156

works out in the woods somewhere. How does it work in an urban environment, when the victim was most likely taken away by car?"

"Finder can find a person lost in the wilderness. Of course, a lot of dogs can do that." Howard reached down unconsciously, resting his hand on top of the dog's head. "Finder can also locate a person in an urban area, with lots of other human scents around. He just needs something with the search object's scent on it."

Special Agent Scott said, "So you're telling me that your dog can track a person that was taken from here in a car."

"No sir, I'm telling you that if that person gets out of that car and Finder is anywhere within two miles of them, he'll pick up their scent."

Keeping the snark out of her voice, Murdoch turned her eyes to Scott and asked, "Have your people come up with anything yet?" Before he could reply she continued, "No, they haven't. If they had you'd be all puffed up telling me about it." Without pausing to take a breath she went on. "So, what's going to happen here is I'm going to go inside Harriet's house and find something from her laundry basket" she placed a hand on Howard's shoulder "and give it to this nice young man so that Finder can start looking for Harriet."

The two men were left alone as Murdoch turned on her heel and entered the house. Moments later she returned. Pulling nitrile gloves from her hands, she handed Howard a plastic evidence bag holding a t-shirt. "And Howard, here's my card. If you find something you can call or text that number."

Howard and Finder moved off toward the street. At the point where it was thought Harriet was forced into the car, Howard held open the bag, allowing Finder a long sniff of its contents.

Resealing the bag, Howard gave Finder the entire thirty feet of lead. The bag was barely sealed when the dog started off at a quick pace down the street and around the corner.

Murdoch watched the dog lift its head and take a long breath. Moments later he moved off at a fast trot.

It's almost as if...No, he couldn't have already picked up her scent. Murdoch sighed, thinking that Laurel was wasting her money. Of course, she has enough money she can afford to waste it.

In less than fifteen minutes Howard and Finder were back at Harriet's house.

With a sneer on his face Special Agent Scott asked, "Lost the trail already?"

"No, actually. We've found her." Not giving Scott time to say anything Howard continued. "There's a blue house two streets west, 589 Hibiscus Street."

Murdoch asked, "How do you know it's the right house?"

Howard turned to her and pulled his phone out. He had a picture of a man getting into a dark gray four-door sedan with Florida tags, he said, "Because this is Harriet's ex-fiancé. She's been running from him for nearly two years now. My guess is that she thought he'd lost her trail and she let her guard down."

Agent Scott narrowed his eyes, studying Howard. "Just how do you know that's her ex-fiancé?"

Ignoring the question Howard closed the phone. "Anyway, he was heading out." Howard shrugged and reached down to rub the top of the dog's head and scratch his ears. "Odds are she's alone in the house, either restrained, drugged, or both."

In a much more civilized tone Murdoch echoed Scott's question. "How do you know who this man is?"

Howard studied Murdoch for a moment as if deciding if or how he was going to answer the question. After several heartbeats he said, "My employer showed me a picture of him and explained how he'd been stalking Harriet." He shrugged. "Guess she thought he'd lost her trail when she decided to settle here."

Special Agent Scott's irritation burst through as he demanded, "Who is your employer, dog boy?"

Murdoch stifled a groan, knowing that any future cooperation from search and rescue dogs in this area would come at a high price, at least if the FBI was asking for the help.

Shaking his head in disbelief Howard gave a slight tug on Finder's lead. "Come on boy. Our work here is done."

Special Agent Scott started to say something, but Murdoch cut him off. "Are you willing to let your ego cost Harriet Walsh her life?"

"Of course not." He glared at her and turned to give orders to his people.

Murdoch's phone pinged with the receipt of a message. Howard had sent her all the pictures he'd taken of the house and its nearby neighbors, the car Alan Henry was driving, and the direction he'd been heading when he left the house. She forwarded the information to Special Agent Scott.

Scott walked to the open back end of his black SUV. On the laptop that was set up he pulled up the street map for the neighborhood.

"If dog boy is right and the abductor went for groceries or even take out, taking into consideration the direction he went when he left the house…"

While Scott was deploying his people to be on the lookout for the abductor's return, Murdoch grabbed Deputies Brighton and Miller.

The trio moved north to the far side of Harriet's neighbor's house, where Murdoch paused and looked between the houses. What she saw brought a smile to her face.

"We're in luck. There are no fences between here and Hibiscus Street." A quick glance back assured her that FBI Special Agent Brian Scott wasn't paying her and her team any attention. She moved off at a slow jog and the two deputies followed her.

When they reached the backyard of the house facing Hibiscus Street, Murdoch stopped. "Wait here."

Staying close to the house she headed toward the street. The Podocarpus at the corner of the house provided her with sufficient cover to get a good look at the blue house across the street. There were no signs of activity. The house had a carport instead of a garage and it was empty.

At the south end of the house Murdoch was using to shield herself from anyone looking out the windows of the target house, was the driveway. On this side of the driveway, near the street was a Viburnum hedge. From what Murdoch could see, she figured if she went to the south side of the house to the south of this one, she wouldn't be seen crossing the street.

Excellent!

Before she re-entered the backyard where Miller and Brighton were waiting for her, she took a deep breath.

Brighton had worked with Murdoch long enough to know she had a plan in mind. He gave her a re-assuring smile. "So, what's the plan, detective?"

Murdoch looked from Brighton to Miller and back. "The plan is very basic and if it works, we make FBI Special Agent Brian Scott look like an idiot and we're heroes. If on the other hand this is the wrong house or anything at all goes wrong with the plan, we could all lose our badges." She paused.

The two deputies exchanged glances, shrugged, turned back to Murdoch, and in stereo said, "I'm good."

Brighton added. "Anything that makes that FBI prick look bad is fine by me."

Murdoch smiled. "In front of this house is a hedge. I want the two of you to go around the north side of this house and wait behind that hedge, until you hear from me. I'm going to go to the south side of the next house over before I cross the street. When I'm in position I'll text you, Brighton." Miller made a face that told her he wasn't happy about Brighton getting the text instead of him.

Boys and their egos. Still, I need him to be on board.

She looked at Miller. "After this is over, assuming we all still have jobs, I'll get your contact info. Right now, we're a bit pressed for time and I already have Brighton's number." This seemed to placate Miller.

Even in the lightweight khakis and polo shirt, running in the Florida heat brought out a light sheen of sweat. Murdoch's regular soft sand runs on the beach had her in shape though and she wasn't even breathing hard when she reached the back of the blue house.

Like many of the houses in the area it was built of concrete block with a large yard. Murdoch remembered this one being available to rent up until about two weeks ago. With her hand on her Glock 22, she moved toward the screened back porch and tried the door. Locked. She pulled her pocketknife and sliced the screening by the door handle, reached inside, and unlocked the door. With the pocketknife back in her pocket, she stepped into the screened room. She tried the sliding glass door and was surprised to find it unlocked. She texted Brighton.

Everything was quiet, not even the birds were chirping, and the ever-present squirrels must be at siesta because they weren't chasing each other through the trees overhead. When she heard running feet approaching the house, she opened the slider enough to step inside.

Inside she cautiously made her way to the front door, turned the deadbolt lock, and opened the door. Murdoch motioned Miller toward the kitchen where a door led to the carport and had Brighton stay near the front door. She headed toward the end of the house with the bedrooms.

On the bed in the master bedroom, she found an unconscious Harriet Walsh. She was curled up in the fetal position. Quickly checking the other bedroom, closets, and the bathroom she hollered out, "Clear. Miller call for an ambulance."

CHAPTER 41

Despite the belief that Alan Henry wasn't coming back to the blue house on Hibiscus Street, Special Agent Scott set up a rotating schedule of agents that stayed at the house just in case he did come back.

After some investigating it was discovered that Brighton and Miller had tripped a motion detector when they stepped onto the front porch. It activated the doorbell camera and Alan Henry was alerted to their presence. The FBI techs rerouted the device's signal to send notifications to a dedicated FBI cell phone, instead of Alan Henry. Agents were assigned shifts at the blue house, no one was happy about it. Special Agent Scott heard that the assignment was considered punishment duty.

In the meantime, Special Agent Scott was sitting in front of his laptop on a video call with his supervisor, FBI Senior Agent Garfield.

"I understand the kidnap victim was rescued by a local LEO." FBI Senior Agent Garfield paused as if looking at a note, but not long enough for Scott to speak. "A woman detective named Murdoch."

"Yes, sir. I was busy setting up a perimeter to capture the man the dog handler said had left the house where he believed the woman was being held."

"With the manpower you had you should have been able to set up your perimeter and send a team to the house at the same time. So, Special Agent Scott explain to me why you didn't do that."

Garfield's even tone was a dead giveaway about how angry he was. The calmer he was in a situation like this the angrier he was. Scott would have preferred that Garfield yell at him.

Swallowing hard Scott replied, "Sir, I didn't believe the dog could have actually found the woman in an urban environment." The words tumbled out of him rapidly, not wanting to give Garfield an opening to speak. "However, to be on the safe side I ordered Det. Murdoch and her two deputies to check out the house. If it turned out to be bad intel, the locals would take the heat."

"Betting against the intel cost you the prestige of rescuing the victim."

"Yes sir, but the important thing was to rescue her, regardless of who got the credit."

Garfield mulled this over for several seconds. "What about the traffic perimeter?"

Scott sighed with relief. He bought it, gullible old fool. "No results there, sir. When the local boys tripped the doorbell camera, the suspect knew better than to come back. Although, I do have agents staying at the target house, just in case."

"Find this man and no more giving away the glory. Understand?"

"Yes, sir."

CHAPTER 42

Murdoch gave up trying to convince Harriet that an overnight stay at the hospital would be a good idea. Having a badge didn't carry a lot of weight with Harriet.

"You can take me to my Cleo, or I'll call a taxi." She shrugged. "Your choice, chère."

Murdoch sighed and looked to the ER doctor for help. The doctor smiled at her and shaking his head said, "Basically, she needs to stay awake until the remainder of the sedative she was given is out of her system. If she has someone with her for the next 24 hours to keep an eye out for any adverse reaction to the stimulant we gave her, she should be fine."

Across the street from the hospital, Alan Henry watched Harriet get into the unmarked patrol car with the female detective. Knowing there were only a few possible destinations and having already decided each one's likelihood, he let the car get out of sight before taking a different route to Laurel Carpenito's beach house.

A short time later he drove past Laurel's house and smiled. As he had anticipated the unmarked patrol car was in the driveway.

He turned west onto the first cross street, Seashell Drive, and pulled into the driveway of the house on the northwest corner of the street. He got out of the car and raised the garage door as if he owned the place. Once the car was inside, he lowered the door.

Feeling pleased with himself about setting up this location in advance he grabbed a beer from the cooler and sat down in the folding chair he'd placed in front of the south facing living room window. From the windowsill he grabbed his binoculars and examined Laurel's house. The sharp angle of the view kept him from being able to see into the house. That didn't bother him because he only needed to know when the detective left and when the house went dark for sleep.

For nearly two years he tracked Harriet, always one or two steps behind her. Now she was within reach and while she was stolen from him earlier in the day, he knew that soon she would be his, forever. He smiled, took a sip of beer, and waited.

CHAPTER 43

When Harriet entered the house Cleo's entire body wiggled and wagged. Harriet squatted down to be at eye level with the Malinois, whose large tongue quickly delivered doggy kisses.

"Yes, I love you too."

While the canine reunion was underway, Murdoch stepped onto the back patio. Surveying the palmettos and the narrow path up from the beach and the many other ways to access Laurel's house from the side and the back, she cursed under her breath.

There's no way to secure this location without a battalion.

Harriet rubbed Cleo's ears, kissed her on top of the head and started to stand up.

As she began to tilt to one side, Laurel moved in to steady her and to Cleo, said, "Mev. Ba'."

Cleo immediately sat.

Harriet gave her a quizzical look. Smiling, Laurel shrugged and as she helped Harriet to a recliner said, "I pay attention. I heard you use those words with Cleo. When I Googled them, I found out they were stay and sit in Klingon." She paused. "I also remember you quietly saying, Skywalker when each new person approached you at the party." She put a pillow behind Harriet's back. "Does that mean that the name of Luke's father would mean to attack?"

Harriet laughed softly and used a hand signal to get Cleo to come. "His name combined with the Klingon word Kapla." Before the last syllable of the word Cleo was alert. Looking around to see if perhaps she had missed something. "Skywalker." Cleo relaxed and laid down next to Harriet's chair.

Murdoch watched the camaraderie between the two women and listened to their easy banter. Moving back into the living room, she said, "I wish I had a couple of Klingon warriors I could leave here with you two." She looked at Laurel. "You're sure I can't convince you to stay in a safe house. Or at least somewhere that's easier to protect than this place."

The look Laurel shot her made Murdoch realize that this was a non-negotiable topic, and she threw her hands up in surrender. "Look, I love this house, but you're very vulnerable here. There are just too many ways for someone to sneak up on this place."

Harriet said, "We have Cleo and…"

Murdoch cut her off. "Not to disparage Cleo but she didn't stop him the last time."

Through gritted teeth Laurel said, "As you've already mentioned this is a different environment. Cleo is inside with us, not out in the yard. And I'm armed."

Murdoch shook her head and sighed. "Please, keep the doors locked, stay inside, and I'll check in on you later."

Laurel walked her to the front door.

"LC, I…"

"Yes, detective."

Looking into those mesmerizing green eyes, Murdoch was suddenly at a brief loss for words. She was tempted to tell Laurel how much she was coming to care about her and that she only wanted to protect her. Then she came back to the real world.

I'm a cop. She's got more money than God and she's still a person of interest in a murder investigation.

Murdoch cleared her throat. "Did you change the code for opening the garage door?" For a split-second Murdoch thought she saw a look of disappointment on Laurel's face.

Laurel schooled her expression to one of mild interest, rather than the disappointment that Murdoch's words hadn't been something more personal.

Somehow, I thought she was…Hell, I don't know what I thought but it certainly wasn't what I got.

"I went one better. I disconnected the door from the opener and threw the metal slide to manually lock it." Anticipating her next question, Laurel continued, "The side door opens out, so I added a hasp and padlock on the inside. I also moved a tall tool chest over to cover the doorway, locked the wheels, and moved the car so close to it that even a cockroach would have a hard time getting in that way."

"Excellent. Now for the important question."

"Yes?"

Looking into Laurel's eyes Murdoch smiled. "Do you actually know how to use that gun?"

"Goodnight, detective." Laurel closed the door and threw the deadbolt.

CHAPTER 44

After locking the front door behind Murdoch, I checked the door to the garage, and the sliding glass doors to the back patio. All was secure.

"Would you like some tea? I get this unique blend from this local lady. She really knows tea."

Harriet smiled. "Yes, I'd love a cup of Lady Anna."

"Coming right... No, I don't have any." I laughed. "Actually, Lady Anna, or more accurately, my running out of Lady Anna is what saved you."

"Really?"

"Yeah, I was really craving some and I was out, so I headed to My Place, but you weren't there and the rest as they say is history."

"So, what do you have to drink?"

"How about some Irish Breakfast tea? It will help keep you awake."

"Sounds good."

I put the tea kettle on the stove. While the water heated, I got out the tea, the brew baskets, the teapot, a cozy for each cup, and the teacups, one of which I nearly dropped when Harriet said, "Do you know how to use that thing?"

"Shit!"

As she tried to keep from laughing, Harriet said, "I'm sorry. I didn't mean to scare you."

Both hands on the edge of the counter I smiled sheepishly. "It's all right. I was just off in my own little world and I thought you were

170

still in the living room. I didn't expect to hear you so close." I took a deep breath and holding Harriet's gaze, continued, "I take it you're referring to the gun."

Harriet nodded.

"Yes. I know how to use it."

The tea kettle whistled. I poured the hot water over the brew baskets in each of the cups and set a timer. Then I placed a cozy over each cup and one over the kettle.

"After Rachel died" it flashed through my mind that that was getting easier to say, "I decided that since I planned on staying solo, I should learn some self-defense." I placed a hand on the holstered 9mm. "This was just one of many classes I indulged in."

My gaze followed Harriet's as she looked at the darkening sky outside. With their nerves already on edge, both women jumped when Cleo barked.

"She needs to go out." I could hear the fear in Harriet's voice.

"Not outside, just to the garage." I looked at the timer on my phone. "How about you carry the tea tray to the living room while I show Cleo her indoor bathroom."

Harriet looked skeptical as I called Cleo to follow me to the garage. At the garage door I said, "The blue and purple cozy is my tea. The other one is yours." Since Cleo showed no hesitation in following me into the garage, Harriet picked up the tea tray and carried it to the living room.

By the time Cleo and I came back in Harriet had set out some cookies for each of us, including treats for Cleo.

I sat down and sipped the hot liquid. For several moments, we sat in companionable silence.

"It's still pretty early and the doctor really doesn't want you going to sleep for a few more hours. How about we watch something funny?" I picked up the remote control. "They say laughter is the best medicine."

"I don't know about laughter being good medicine. I do know that having a friend like you is – well, I don't have the words for it." She fixed her eyes on mine. "Det. Murdoch told me about the bloodhound. If you hadn't…" She took a deep breath. "Anyway, please let me know how much it cost. I want to pay you back. I know it had to be expensive."

I leaned forward in my chair without breaking eye contact. "Do you know who Larissa Carpenter is?"

Harriet looked confused. "Of course, a while back she and her partner won that huge lottery jackpot. What does that have to do with what we're talking about?"

I sighed. "My name isn't Laurel Carpenito. I am Larissa Carpenter." The words poured out of me not giving her a chance to respond. "Det. Murdoch knows and has agreed that as long as my identity isn't relevant to the investigation, she'll keep it to herself." I smiled. "I've asked her to just call me by my initials, LC, that way she's not overtly keeping my identity a secret."

Harriet was quiet for a few minutes. "I appreciate you trusting me enough to tell me this. However, I don't see what relevance that has."

Shaking my head, a small laugh escaped me. "Harriet, what I paid for the search team was nothing compared to how highly I value your friendship."

CHAPTER 45

I looked at the number on my cell phone and sighed. A call from the Sheriff was never a good thing.

"Murdoch."

"Your office now." The call ended.

Definitely not a good thing. The Sheriff didn't often come over here from the main office and when he did it was never a good thing.

At least he won't have time to stew about whatever it was that had him riled up, since I was just parking my car in the sub-station parking lot when the call came in.

I suppose that FBI Special Agent Brian Scott is the reason I'm about to have my head handed to me. I wonder if he'll be there in person... No, he strikes me as more a written complaint kind of guy.

Outside my office door, I took a deep breath, knocked, and opened the door. For a moment I stood in the open doorway, surprised to see FBI Special Agent Amber Hoffner sitting across from Sheriff Whitaker, who was seated at my desk.

"Close the door Murdoch." The Sheriff had an unusually deep voice for such a skinny fellow.

Without a word I closed the door and walked to stand next to the empty chair beside the one Special Agent Hoffner occupied.

Time on the force taught me to just keep my mouth shut until spoken to when being called in for a chewing out. It was best to make sure what the problem was before offering explanations or defenses.

"I understand you two have met."

"Yes, sir. I've met Special Agent Hoffner on a variety of occasions."

Amber nodded her agreement.

I shifted my weight, knowing I shouldn't sit down until the Sheriff offered me a seat. However, I very much wanted to get down on the same level with Amber. It would make it so much easier to get a read on what was going on, if I could look her in the eyes and see her facial expressions.

"Stop fidgeting and sit down, detective."

"Yes, sir." I stepped to the front of the chair and lowered myself into it.

"Tell me about this Harriet Walsh case. What happened out there?"

There was no doubt in my mind that Sheriff Whitaker knew exactly what had happened. He wanted to see if I would give him an honest answer.

I cleared my throat, took a deep breath, and dove in headfirst. "...After Mr. Barlow left with Finder, I realized that FBI Special Agent Scott had no intention of acting on the information the dog handler had provided beyond setting up a net to catch Alan Henry when he returned, if he returned." I licked my lips and continued, "I ordered Deputies Miller and Brighton to come with me. We cut through yards and came to the house the dog handler had said Mr. Henry left from. The three of us entered the house, found Ms. Walsh, and called for an ambulance. Ms. Walsh had been sedated with something to keep her quiet. The ambulance transported her to the hospital. The doctor examined her and released her, with the order that she have someone with her for the next 24-hours. Just to make sure there were no serious after affects from the drugs she'd been given." Glancing from the Sheriff to Amber and back I finished. "I left her with Laurel Carpenito, at Ms. Carpenito's beach house. I told them I'd stop in later tonight and see how they're doing."

The Sheriff and Amber exchanged glances.

"What?" I looked back and forth between the two. "What's going on here?"

The Sheriff gave an almost imperceptible nod to Amber, who turned to me. "The doctor had to give Ms. Walsh a stimulant to counteract the sedatives Har...Ms. Walsh was given. If she hadn't received medical care as quickly as she did, this might have turned into a homicide investigation."

"Shit!" I looked from the Sheriff to Amber. "Apologies for the language, sir."

Sheriff Whitaker waved away such minor concerns.

Amber laughed softly. "No worries. I believe that was pretty much my response when I heard that bit of news."

"I remember the doctor mentioning that she had to be aware of any adverse reaction to a stimulant that he administered. I had no idea that..." I took a deep breath and studied Amber as I asked, "Is there any evidence tying any of the criminal activity in Coventry Beach to the FBI's human trafficking case?"

Amber didn't speak but her facial expression told me everything I needed to know. "Which case? Natalie Kramer?" Amber touched her index finger to the tip of her nose. "Really, her murder is somehow tied to the traffickers."

I knew my anger was showing in my voice, but I was too frustrated to care. "How is it tied? Do you think she was working with them? Did she see something she wasn't supposed to see? Hear something?" I paused and rubbed the back of my neck. "I'm sorry Amb...Special Agent Hoffner. I'm not angry with you. It's the

175

situation. I don't know if I'm helping your investigation or harming it because I don't have sufficient information."

Amber pursed her lips. straightened her posture and rested her arms on the chair arms. She moved her gaze from me to Sheriff Whitaker and back to me. "We think that the victim, Natalie Kramer, interrupted a turtle nest robbery. The only way we know her murder is tied to the traffickers is because the gun used to kill her, is the same gun that was used...in a murder we know was committed by one of the trafficker's henchmen." She sighed. "We have no idea how the theft of turtle eggs is connected."

Connecting the turtle egg robberies to the human traffickers was an angle I'd been thinking about for a while. "Are these traffickers bringing people in or taking people out of the country?"

"Both."

I thought about that for a moment. "Then most likely they're also supplying someone along their route with the eggs."

Amber's look of confusion prompted me to continue. "Turtle eggs are considered a delicacy in some parts of the world."

"How do you know this?"

"After Natalie Kramer's murder I did some research." I shook my head. "The price per egg is only three to five dollars. Not enough money to offset the risk. At least not for someone making thousands from selling people."

Leaning forward I said, "You said the gun was used by a low-level member of the crew in a previous case."

"Yeah." Amber suddenly realized where I was headed with this line of thought. "You think a couple of the low-level guys decided to pick up some extra money on the side."

"Somewhere along their route they've come across someone with a desire for turtle eggs." I shrugged. "Why not use the boss's network to make a little extra money? I mean, it's not taking money from the boss. He's not about to traffic in penny ante turtle eggs."

Amber shook her head in disbelief. "No, he's not going to bother with turtle eggs. There's not enough return on investment."

Sheriff Whitaker said, "That's all very interesting; however, it doesn't help us solve the murders here in Coventry Beach." He stood up. "And it doesn't do anything to help the FBI with their human traffickers."

I stood and glanced at the wall clock. "No sir. I should be checking in on Ms. Walsh and Ms. Carpenito. We still haven't picked up Alan Henry."

Amber rose from her chair. "How about if I ride along with you and we can discuss ideas on how we might be able to help each other with our respective cases?" Amber paused and smiled at the Sheriff. "With your permission, Sheriff Whitaker."

Sheriff Whitaker nodded and returned to my desk chair. In his thick southern drawl, he added, "I've never seen an FBI Agent so accommodating to local law enforcement as you, Special Agent Hoffner. Perhaps this younger generation will be the beginning of a more cooperative alliance between the FBI and local agencies."

CHAPTER 46

Neither of the two women spoke until they were in Murdoch's car.

"Where's Special Agent Scott? I mean I figured if I was going to find anyone in there it would be him."

Amber sighed. "Yes, well, he's gotten himself in a... situation with the higher ups. They don't like it when one of ours is shown up by a local."

Murdoch smiled as she pulled out of the parking lot. "Especially when that local is female."

Amber laughed. "I can't say the gender thing is an issue with the higher ups, but I know it bugs the hell out of Scott."

Amber studied Murdoch as she maneuvered the car into traffic. Murdoch was aware of the scrutiny but said nothing until they were stopped at a red-light. Then she turned to face Amber. "Do I pass?"

"What do..." Amber blushed and looked away. "I'm sorry. I didn't mean to stare. It's just..."

"Just what?" The light turned green and Murdoch pulled away. "Yes, I'm a lesbian, if that's what you're wondering."

"No, I figured that part out some time back." She smiled. "The first time I saw you and Laris...Laurel together." She paused. "Why does it bother you so when I mention Laurel?"

"What makes you think it bothers me?"

"Oh, I don't know, maybe the death grip you have on the steering wheel."

Murdoch tried to relax her grip and changed the topic. "We're going to cruise the area a bit before we stop at Ms. Carpenito's house" was her only response.

"Sure."

They both scanned the houses and cars in the neighborhood. There was nothing out the ordinary along Atlantic Avenue.

As they turned west on Seashell Drive, Amber asked, "Is it common around here for the light to be on in a garage while the rest of the house is dark?"

"Which house?"

"On the corner my side."

Murdoch stopped the car and adjusted the rearview mirror to get a look at the house in question. "Was there a for sale sign in the yard?"

"Not that I saw."

Murdoch backed up, turned off the headlights and pulled into the driveway. She walked around the car and stepped into the yard, with Amber right behind her. Aiming her flashlight down she explored the dying greenery and soon found the for-sale sign that had been tossed into the bushes.

Murdoch led the way back to the driveway and stopped in front of the garage door.

She turned to Amber, who was right beside her and said, "Cover me." Murdoch bent down, grabbed the rope that was sticking out from under the door, and pulled the door up.

Stepping back so that she wouldn't be hit by the rising garage door – Amber drew her sidearm.

The hinges were well-oiled and made little noise as the door went up. Murdoch released the rope, drew her gun, and flashlight. "Sheriff's Department. Anybody home?"

179

The light source was an LED bar light attached to the circuit breaker box by magnets. Other than that, the only thing in the garage was a dark gray four door sedan. The car and the tags matched what Alan Henry was last seen driving. Murdoch placed a hand on the hood. The engine was cold.

Guns and flashlights leading the way the two women entered the house and quickly determined no one was home.

Murdoch looked out the window where the chair and cooler were set up. She didn't need to pick up the binoculars sitting on the windowsill to know which house was being watched.

"Shit!" She shone her flashlight on the beer can sitting on top of the cooler. Beads of water were still running down the sides of the can.

She tapped her earpiece and said, "Dispatch." Her phone automatically dialed the station.

"County dispatch, how may..."

"This is Murdoch. Get someone to 4578 Seashell Drive in Coventry Beach. Kidnapping suspect Alan Henry's car is in the garage. He's been watching Laurel Carpenito's house at 12308 Atlantic Avenue. Special Agent Hoffner and I are headed to Carpenito's house now. My car will be in the driveway here, we'll be on foot."

Before she could disconnect the dispatcher said, "Det. Murdoch, I'll get someone there as soon as I can, but it could be a while. Right now, the closest unit to you is thirty minutes away. Everyone else is tied up on calls."

"Great. Let the Sheriff know what's going on and get me some backup as soon as possible."

She ended the call and moved past Amber, who was on her phone. In the garage she lifted the hood of the car and pulled loose every spark plug wire she could lay her hands on.

Amber entered the garage as she lowered the hood of the car. "Brian...Special Agent Scott has been brought up-to-date. It'll take him at least thirty minutes to get here. What's the plan?"

Mentally reviewing all the approaches to the beach house, Murdoch replied, "Since it's just the two of us, I think I'll just go to the front door, ring the bell, and see what happens." Smiling she added, "I want you to go through the neighbor's yard and come up from the beach."

Amber shook her head in disbelief. "In other words, we're flying by the seat of our pants."

Still smiling, Murdoch shrugged. "Sometimes you just have to improvise. Oh yeah, and backup is about thirty minutes away."

"Of course it is."

CHAPTER 47

Alan Henry was coming up from the beach to Laurels house.

From the edge of the path leading to Laurel's house Edith Bates had watched his progress. Curious about who he was and what he was up to she waited for him.

He thought he heard something behind him but before he could turn around something cold and hard was pressed against the base of his skull.

"Don't move. Who are you and what are you doing here?"

He licked his lips, calculating the odds of overpowering his captor. "I could ask you the same thing."

"You could if you were holding a gun to my head. But you're not – I'm the one in control, so I get to ask the questions and you get to answer them." Alan started to raise his arms, as if he were surrendering. "I told you not to move." Edith planted a foot to the back of his right knee. He staggered and while he was off balance, she forced him to his knees.

Alan knew this woman wasn't the detective and she wasn't the woman holding Harriet captive. "My name is Alan Henry."

"Alright, Alan Henry. What are you doing here?"

"I've come to rescue Harriet, so that she and I can be together."

It didn't take long for Edith and Alan to decide they could work together, and they would both get what they wanted.

CHAPTER 48

Laurel heard a sound at the sliding glass doors. "Harriet, get upstairs. Take Cleo and Tut with you." She looked Harriet in the eyes. "Don't come down until I give you the all clear. No matter what you hear, stay upstairs."

Harriet nodded her agreement. She scooped Tut from the back of the recliner and headed upstairs. Once Harriet and the dog were out of sight, Laurel moved to the sliding glass door.

Laurel moved the blinds aside and looked out the sliding glass door to see Edith Bates holding a gun to a man's head. It was Alan Henry.

"Open the door or I'll kill him right now."

"You think I care? My biggest concern will be getting the blood cleaned up."

Keeping Alan Henry in front of her like a shield, Bates aimed her gun at Laurel. "Then how about if I just shoot you. Even through the glass, I can't miss at this range. You've got 5 seconds."

She's right about that, at this range there's no way she can miss. Have to buy time. Murdoch said she'd be stopping by to check on us. Just have to hope she shows up before this crazy bitch kills me.

Laurel unlocked the door and moved back.

Bates whispered something in Alan Henry's ear. "Cover my back. When I'm finished with this one, you can have your precious Harriet." She released him. As soon as she let him go, he moved toward the path to the beach and was swallowed by the dark.

Bates stepped into the house with her gun still aimed at Laurel. "Put your gun on the bar and back away from it."

Laurel had her hands in the air. "What makes you think I have a gun?"

"Because I know all about you, Ms. Larissa Carpenter. I know about your money and I know you're the busy body that reported me to the cops for killing that cheating scumbag of a husband. Now put your gun on the bar and back away from it."

Laurel slowly reached behind her and pulled her gun from its holster. She placed it on the bar and took a couple of small steps back.

Bates smiled. "Further back."

CHAPTER 49

As Murdoch stepped onto Laurel Carpenito's property the security lights made the entire front of the house, as bright as day. Before she could ring the doorbell, she heard the door unlock. Murdoch took a deep breath and opened the door.

Across the room Edith Bates stood behind Laurel with gun in hand. "Hello Mrs. Bates."

Edith Bates snarled. "Think you're pretty smart, don't you?"

"Smarter than the last cop that crossed paths with you. I know you're dangerous. That idiot thought he was going to walk over to your house, arrest you, and get you to confess to two murders. I have no such illusion."

"Humph. So, what do you think is going to happen? Huh? You think just because you're a woman I'll surrender."

Murdoch continued to slowly move across the living room as she spoke. "No, I figure I'll have to kill you."

Edith laughed. "I'll give you points for hutzpah. But I'm pretty sure I'll be the one doing the killing, you" she pointed the gun at Laurel's head "and your pretty little friend here, too."

"Well, that's just a chance I'll have to take. You know when it's your job to serve and ..."

"Stop! Right there, not another step or I'll kill her now."

Murdoch dropped her foot back to the ground. "What method do you have in mind for Miss Busy Body here? I know how creative you like to be with your killing, Mrs. Bates." Murdoch forced a smile of approval. "I was there when they dug up Ariel Fenton. That was pure Machiavelli."

Gunshots from the beach drew Edith's attention. Murdoch and Laurel both took advantage of the distraction. Murdoch dove at Edith, as Laurel twisted away from her captor.

Murdoch tackled Bates with her hands on the woman's shoulders and allowed her momentum to take them both to the floor. Her hands still on Bates' shoulders she pulled the woman toward her and then slammed her to the tile floor. The resounding crack of skull on tile was audible. Edith Bates lay still.

Murdoch grabbed Bates' gun, looked around and saw that Laurel was safe. She still didn't know where Harriet was, but her immediate concern was the gunfire from the beach. "Stay here!" Murdoch tucked Bates' gun into her waistband, pulled her own weapon, and headed for the sliding glass door.

"Wait, these will help you see out there." Laurel handed her a pair of night vision goggles.

"Thanks." Before she opened the slider, she said, "Keep an eye on her. If she looks like she's going to get up off the floor" she smiled "don't let her." Without another word Murdoch was out the door.

She slipped the goggles on and immediately the black night became less forbidding. Everything looked like an old black and white movie.

A faint voice called her name. Stepping to the head of the sandy path that led to the beach, she could see Amber lying on the path. Scanning the immediate area for any threats, she moved as quickly as possible to Amber's side. The FBI agent was still conscious, but she was losing a lot of blood.

Keeping her ears and eyes open for whoever had shot Amber, Murdoch called dispatch again. "Officer down. I need an ambulance at 12308 Atlantic. Better send two, I also have an injured suspect."

"I think I hit him. Surprised me. Knew you had a perp in the house. Didn't realize there were two of them."

"Is she going to be all right?" Laurel's voice from the top of the trail startled Murdoch.

"I thought I told you to stay inside."

"It's all right. I left Harriet to guard Bates."

"I need something to stop the bleeding." Before the sound of the last syllable had been taken by the sea breeze, Laurel peeled out of her t-shirt and handed it to Murdoch.

"I'll be back in a minute with towels." Murdoch watched Laurel disappear into the house.

Amber looked at her and said, "You gotta love a woman who'll give you the shirt off her back."

"Hmmm. You need to be quiet and lie still until the ambulance gets here."

*   *   *   *   *

Sheriff Whitaker's driver, Deputy Danielle Shaw, pulled into the driveway of 4578 Seashell Drive, next to Murdoch's car. The headlights of the patrol car swept across Alan Henry's body, lying on the driveway in front of the garage door.

Deputy Shaw got out of the patrol car. She checked Henry's neck for a pulse. "He's been shot but he's still alive."

Sheriff Whitaker grabbed the radio mike. "This is Sheriff Whitaker, we need an ambulance at 4578 Seashell Drive, Coventry Beach. We have a gunshot victim."

187

CHAPTER 50

When FBI Special Agent Brian Scott arrived at Laurel's house, an ambulance was pulling away. Inside the house, Laurel, Harriet, and Murdoch were sitting at the kitchen bar. On the kitchen floor was a body covered with a sheet.

Murdoch watched the color drain from Special Agent Scott's face, as he stared at the shrouded form. He turned his gaze to Murdoch. "Where's Am...Special Agent Hoffner?"

Murdoch walked over to him. "She's in the ambulance that just left."

"Thank God." He turned for the door but stopped and asked, "Who's that?"

"Edith Bates."

Scott nodded and headed for the door.

Murdoch called after him. "They're taking her to Coventry General. It was a through and through, she's going to be fine."

Smiling she returned to her stool at the kitchen bar. "There may be hope for that boy yet."

CHAPTER 51

Laurel, Murdoch, and Harriet were at My Place waiting for FBI Special Agents Scott and Hoffner to stop in on their way out of town.

"So Detective, what's the status on Harriet's stalker?" Laurel knew that Harriet wanted to ask the question but was afraid to hear the answer.

Looking up from studying her coffee, Murdoch moved her gaze from Laurel to Harriet, who seemed to be holding her breath. "Unless he comes back from the dead, Alan Henry won't bother anyone again."

A smile spread across Harriet's face. "Oh, but it's so wrong to be happy about the death of anyone." She sighed. "Still, now I can breathe again." A big smile split her face. "And even better I don't have to leave Coventry Beach."

The rental car with FBI Special Agents Amber Hoffner and Brian Scott pulled into the parking lot ending the discussion of Alan Henry.

While they were all certain that Amber would be cleared in the shooting death of Alan Henry, no one knew how she was handling the fact that she had killed a man. So, it wasn't a topic anyone was going to bring up.

Harriet met the two FBI agents at the door with a hug. "Thank you, Special Agent Hoffner and you too Special Agent Scott, for all of your help." Harriet's thick New Orleans accent was more pronounced than normal, as her eyes glistened with unshed tears of relief. "Everyone needs to sit down. I'll fix a great breakfast. French Toast, Beignets, strawberries, and chicory coffee."

Scott smiled, "As much as we would love to stay and eat, we have to get back to DC and we're driving. The doctor said it wasn't a good idea for Amb... Special Agent Hoffner to fly just yet." He smiled at Amber. "However, she insisted we stop by on our way out of town."

Murdoch extended her hand to Special Agent Scott. "I suppose you'll be back before long. After all you haven't closed your case yet."

Special Agent Scott shook her hand. "No, we haven't closed the case and odds are it will be assigned to another agent." He smiled. "I'm getting a promotion. I'll be heading up a field office out west."

Congratulations came from all present.

Murdoch silently marveled at the inner workings of the FBI. One minute he's in trouble with his superiors and the next he gets a promotion. Go figure.

"If you ever make it out to Idaho Falls, stop by and say hello."

Laurel looked at Amber. "What about you, Amber? Are you going to continue to do field work or are you headed back to your keyboard?"

"I'm not sure." Amber laughed at the look of surprise on Laurel's face. "I know. You would think after getting shot, I'd be happy to get back to a computer" her tone was thoughtful as she continued "but I'm not sure if that's what I want. Time will tell. Besides, in the agency, it's not always up to you where you go." She paused, "I'll miss all of you and I will definitely miss your Lady Anna tea, Harriet."

Moments later the two FBI agents were in their rental car with cups of Lady Anna and a bag of Madeleines.

Murdoch had walked the two FBI agents to their car. As she watched them drive away, she had a feeling that Amber Hoffner was going to be fine. She had been concerned about how well the young woman would deal with having killed a man but now she was certain that she would adjust to that reality with little trouble.

She turned to go back inside the café, but before she reached the door, Carly Reddington pulled into the parking lot. Murdoch waited for her to get out of the car.

"Hello, Murdoch." Carly stood just inside the open door of the driver's side.

The detective walked across the parking lot.

"Carly. What brings you out so early?" It was common knowledge that Carly was more a night owl than an early bird. "Why don't you come in for a cup of coffee?"

"I have a plane to catch." She paused as if expecting Murdoch to say something, when she made no comment, Carly continued, "I have to follow the story. Besides, I'm certain you would rather I was bothering some other detective, instead of hanging around here hounding you about Natalie's murder."

Carly held out a business card. "I can be reached at that number, no matter where I am in the world, I'll get the message."

Murdoch examined the card and then looked at Carly. "I'll let you know when we catch Natalie's killer."

Carly looked past her at the two women in the café. She smiled and waved at them before returning her attention to Murdoch. "You do know that Larissa Carpenter likes you, don't you?"

Blushing slightly Murdoch changed the subject. "When did you learn her real name?"

Carly laughed as she got back into her rental car. "A reporter never reveals her sources." From the driver's seat she smiled up at Murdoch. "If you can't figure out that that woman is interested in you, you're not much of a detective, Murdoch."

Watching Carly drive away gave Murdoch some time to get her thoughts in order before going back into the café. She was barely in the door when Laurel asked, "How come Carly didn't come inside?"

"She has a plane to catch."

"But she took the time to stop by and give you her number."

The two women were smiling at her and exchanging knowing glances. But there was something about Laurel's tone of voice that seemed off for a general ribbing.

Maybe Carly's right. No! Even if she is right, I can't be getting involved with the number one suspect in Natalie Kramer's murder. Even if I don't think she did it, there's still the possibility that she's involved.

"It's not what you're thinking." Murdoch waved the card at them. "She just wanted to make sure I could reach her so that when I catch Natalie's killer, I can let her know."

LC watched Murdoch put the business card in a pocket. It doesn't really matter if she's got a thing going on with Carly or not. Her only interest in me is in relation to Natalie Kramer's murder.

CHAPTER 52

Later that night, Tut and I were sitting on the back deck as the sun sank in the western sky behind us. Sipping my tea and rubbing Tuts' ears, I breathed a sigh of mild relief. Relief that was tinged with concern.

Harriet is safe. The mystery of Amber Hoffner re-entering my life is solved. I suppose eventually I'll forgive her for lying to me. Edith Bates is dead. However, I'm still a person of interest in Natalie Kramer's murder.

With a soft slight smile, I considered this last issue. At least it gives Murdoch a reason to stay in touch with me.

About The Author

A native Floridian, Darlene has moved away multiple times, only to be drawn back by the smell of the sea, the sun, and the feel of sand between her toes. She and her spouse live near Darlene's hometown of Daytona Beach.

At the time of this writing, they have one rescue cat named Keke. She's part Russian Blue and quite often Darlene believes the cat is channeling a dog. Keke loves to follow her around and sit on the floor near her chair while she writes.

OTHER BOOKS IN THIS SERIES

Lust & Distrust
A Larissa Carpenter Mystery #2

Since moving to Coventry Beach, Larissa Carpenter hasn't found life in the small beach town to provide the tranquility she expected. Not wanting everyone in town to know that she's the Larissa Carpenter who won one of the state's largest lottery jackpots, she goes by Laurel Carpenito or LC.

Being a person of interest in two murder cases, one of which still hasn't been solved, is most unsettling and it's not the only unsettling thing in LC's life. Her attraction to Detective Angela Murdoch and the feeling that she's being followed are the other disconcerting issues.

Unsure of who's following her, LC wonders if her former high school classmate, FBI Special Agent Amber Hoffner has something to do with it.

Does the FBI think she's involved in the human trafficking ring? Does Detective Murdoch think she killed Natalie Kramer? Is Detective Murdoch attracted to her or is that a figment of her imagination?

Is LC right about being followed? If so, who is it? The FBI? The local police? Someone else?

Fatal Misunderstanding
A Larissa Carpenter Mystery #3

Follow Larissa Carpenter and four friends on a pre-All Hallows Eve girls' weekend in the mystic town of Cerridwen. The fun comes to an end with the discovery of a dead witch in a cottage in the woods and suspicions about at least one of the women begins. It turns out that the dead woman is the former lover of Larissa Carpenter's current friend with benefits. After spending weeks avoiding Det. Angela Murdoch, Larissa is forced to call her.

"Ms. Carpenter, you report more dead bodies to me than the 911 dispatcher," said Det. Angela Murdoch.

OTHER BOOKS BY THIS AUTHOR

The Legend of Erin Foster

Available as Kindle and Paperback

The Order for Morality and Justice has grown its power base and now reaches to the highest level of government. Virtually all civil rights laws are gone. The federal government is on the verge of declaring martial law nationwide.

Warrants are issued daily for the arrest of enemies of the state. When they come for Erin Foster and her partner of seven years, Alice, the Peacekeeper of The Order for Morality and Justice shoots out the front door lock. His bullet ricochets and kills Alice.

Alice's death flips a switch in Erin Foster and her mission to destroy The Order and its leader, The Reverend James Calton III, begins. In her eyes, you're either part of the solution or you're part of the problem.

Life Is Full of Surprises

What do industrial espionage, an unsolved hit and run and a bloody knife in an ice cream carton have in common? They're all elements in the romantic mystery Life Is Full of Surprises.

Barbara Orlock and Judy Langdon have both sworn off falling in love. They agree their relationship will be no strings attached, just fun and games.

Judy's ex-lover, Carol Engram, is found dead in Judy's apartment. Actin on an anonymous tip police search Barbara's freezer and find the murder weapon, a bloody knife, hidden in an ice cream carton.

Will Barbara's faith in her business associate, Gerald, be her undoing? Was the death of Barbara's previous lover, Linda, really an accident? Who has the most to gain by Carol's death? Or maybe the question should be who has the most to gain if Barbara is convicted of Carol's murder? Can Judy unravel the mystery and clear Barbara of murder?

The Origin of Deanna Dorak
Nedamla Book #1

Is she merely a freak of nature…or is she from another world?

Deanna Dorak suddenly finds herself alone in the world and begins to realize that it may not even be her world. With confusing images forcing their way into her consciousness she struggles to understand who she is and why she's here. She elicits the help of her best friend and former lover, Kate, who believes that all of Deanna's problems stem from her inability to accept her mother's death. That is until she sees the gills that have begun to form on Deanna's sides. Kate brings Deanna to Dr. Jason Alexander, who vows to help her and protect her from government scientists.

Soon after, Kate's body is pulled from the river – someone broke her neck.

A frantic search for answers takes Deanna on the quest of her life. Is she the reason her friend was killed? Is Jason friend or foe? Is he holding her captive for his own scientific research? Is she really from another planet, an underwater world inhabited only by women? Can she trust the detective assigned to solve Kate's murder? Can she trust herself?

Aneesha's Prophecy
Nedamla Book #2

*"The daughter will return and avenge the death of her mother
and those innocents killed here today."*

Dorak Deanna has come home to claim her birthright. Home, to a
planet she remembers only through the implanted memories of her
mother, Miktra. Home to a planet still occupied by the same Empyrean
forces that forced her departure nearly thirty years ago.

The Day of Ascension is fast approaching and the Empyrean Governor
of Nedamla grows more fearful of Aneesha's Prophecy with each
passing day. Especially since each day seems to bring another
unexplained, violent death of at least one of his soldiers. Yet the
Empyror refuses his requests for more troops, assuring him that since
Aneesha's child was killed during the invasion, there is no heir to
ascend to the throne.

By accident Deanna discovers she has the ability to communicate, with
at least one Nedamlan, by using only her thoughts. Is it possible that
there are others among her people with this ability? Perhaps it will be
the secret weapon she needs.

Even with the ability to mind-talk, how can one woman turn a population
of women, known for their pacifism, into warriors? And if she and her
warriors take Nedamla from the troops now occupying her, how will they
maintain their freedom? The Empyror has more than enough troops to
simply send another invasion force.

As if fighting the Empyre weren't enough to worry about, Deanna has
another problem – she has fallen in love.

Will Deanna fulfill Aneesha's Prophecy? Can she return her people to a
time when they were fierce warriors, asking no quarter and giving
none? Will Jorsta agree to join with her?